SPOTTING
THE FIRE

NEW FREEDOM FIRE AND RESCUE

LILY J. HANN

eBook ASIN: B0F253KJCC

Paperback ISBN: 979-8-9998628-0-8

Published by: Lily Hann, Maryland, USA

Cover Design by: Madisyn, Mountain Peak Editorial

Edited by: Madisyn, Mountain Peak Editorial

Contents

Dedication   1

Prologue   3

Chapter 1   5

Chapter 2   15

Chapter 3   27

Chapter 4   40

Chapter 5   53

Chapter 6   66

Chapter 7   79

Chapter 8   92

Chapter 9   105

Chapter 10   114

Chapter 11   128

Chapter 12   141

Chapter 13   155

Chapter 14   168

Chapter 15   182

Chapter 16   196

Chapter 17   209

Chapter 18   222

Chapter 19   235

Chapter 20   248

Chapter 21   260

Epilogue   271

Sneak Peek from Flare Up   280

About the author   283

Also by Lily Hann   284

To the members at Company 33, thank you for your service to our community.

So do not fear, for I am with you; do not be dismayed, for I am your God.
Isaiah 41:10 (NIV)

Prologue

*T*HE CRAFTONS WOULD BE *dealt with by the end of the day.*

Eros's promise was still displayed on the phone. If he didn't take care of them, there would be others more competent to do that kind of work. Eros was simply the closest.

Malinoe huffed and typed a reply. W*hat of the package?*

The man-child was losing his touch if he couldn't procure a simple package.

Malinoe leaned back into the plush leather office chair. Charles Crafton was persistent for an old guy, but Malinoe wouldn't underestimate any man who tried to stop them. Former spies or not, they would both die today.

The office door opened slowly as Pyroeis entered.

"You wanted to see me?" he said in a dead voice.

"Yes, go to New Freedom to check on Eros. If he fails, get rid of him and bring me the package."

Pyroeis gave a curt nod and left.

The man was obsessed with fire, but he was a good soldier.

The computer program was as good as theirs, and the men in DC would be satisfied. It was wise to have people in power to owe you something.

Chapter 1

W ALKING ACROSS THE HANGAR to the locker room, after dropping the papers in the office first, Scott Crafton stripped off his flight jumpsuit, showered, and placed all of his things in his Airman Battle Uniform—ABU—duffel bag. He closed his locker and turned to leave when a familiar voice grabbed his attention.

"Are you sure I can't persuade you to stay? I have reenlistment paperwork with me." The colonel's gravelly voice filled the locker room. Scott came to attention and saluted his commanding officer. Returning the salute, Colonel Yates gave a half smile. "At ease, Sergeant. You are officially no longer under my command."

Scott came to rest at ease. His military training was too much a part of who he was now to forgo the formalities. "To answer your question, sir, I'm sure. I accepted the job as fire chief back home. It will be a good change." He said this to remind himself as much as to reassure his commanding officer that this was the right decision.

"In that case, it's been a pleasure, Crafton." The colonel extended his hand. "If you change your mind, we'll gladly take you back. You have my number if you ever need something."

After saluting one last time, Scott left the hangar and headed for his truck. It would be a few hours before he reached New Freedom. Plenty of time to decompress, compartmentalize, and come up with something to say to his dad. He had forgiven the man years ago, but he wasn't sure if his father would even speak to him.

He tossed his bag in the back seat of his truck and climbed in. As he turned over the engine, his phone rang. His mom's name popped up on the screen. He connected his phone to his truck and picked up.

"Hey, Mom, I'm..."

"Scott, listen to me." Screeching tires came across the line along with his mother's terse greeting.

Immediately on alert, Scott put his truck into gear. "Where are you?"

"We are on highway fourteen. Two exits past the cabin. Heading south. Dad spotted our tail, and I'm trying to lose them." The engine revved as she continued. "Scott, you need to protect Rachel from them. Go to the cabin." Then a word he rarely heard her use flew from his mother's mouth, followed by the crunching of metal.

"Mom! Dad!" His desperate shouts reverberated through the cab of his truck.

No response. Punching the hold button, he dialed the dispatch number for New Freedom, which he had only programmed into his phone this morning.

"New Freedom dispatch, what's your emergency?" The calm voice pushed back the tension in him.

Scott gave the orders as he pulled away from the base. "This is Scott Crafton, the new fire chief. There has been a possible multiple motor vehicle collision fifteen miles north of town on Highway 14. Two known victims. Male, fifty-eight, and female, fifty-five. Send police to secure the scene before EMS arrives."

"Yes, sir." A slight pause. "Emergency crews and police are on their way. Are you on scene?"

"No, I was talking with them on the phone. My ETA to the scene is two hours. I need to go. I have their line on hold. I'm going to try and make contact again."

Without waiting for a reply, Scott switched calls back to his mom's line. "Mom? Dad? Can either of you hear me?"

Silence kicked his adrenaline into higher gear.

Scott took a shaking breath. "I sent emergency crews and police your way. They should be there in about fifteen minutes. If you can hear me, please say something."

A muffled sound followed by a grunt made hope bubble inside, calming his heart a fraction.

"Scott." The voice was weak, but it was unmistakably his father's. "I'm sorry."

Those words caused a coughing fit.

"Don't try to speak, Dad. We can talk when I get there." Scott choked the words out. The one thing he had been dreading all day was now the only thing he desperately wanted.

"Take care of Rachel and your mom, if she wakes up." Charles Crafton was always a strong man. To hear his inability to breathe pushed Scott to go even faster. "You were right, son. Please forgive me. I've always loved you, and I'm proud of who you've become."

Scott never thought he would see the day when he heard those words.

Police sirens were getting louder in the background. "Help is on the way, Dad. You stay alive and we'll work all this out." Scott swallowed the sudden lump in his throat. "I forgive you and love you, too."

Scott prayed that whoever arrived on scene would be able to keep them alive long enough for him to make it to New Freedom.

He heard a voice calling for them. Scott said goodbye, hung up, and dialed someone he hadn't spoken to in over a decade.

"Jamison."

"Tylan. It's Scott Crafton. I have a situation. I need you to get to my parents' cabin and get eyes on Rachel for me." Scott filled him in briefly on what happened.

Being one of the few people who actually knew the truth about his family, Tylan didn't even hesitate. "Do you know if her location was compromised?"

"I have no idea. We have to assume the worst until you can prove otherwise." Scott blew out a breath. His baby sister needed him. His parents needed him.

"It's fine. I'll take some backup." Tylan opened his car door.

"No." Scott didn't want to involve more people until he could figure out what his parents were caught up in.

"If I'm walking into a hostage or kidnapping situation, it'll be better for everyone involved if I have help." Tylan's command and logic left little room for argument.

"Fine. Call me back when you get there with a sitrep."

"Done," Tylan agreed.

"And, Tylan, thanks. I owe you one."

Tylan grunted in acknowledgement as he slammed the door shut and revved the engine as the call disconnected. Scott blinked back tears and did the only thing he could think to do. He prayed.

"You keep looking at that phone like you are expecting your hot date to call." Her partner, who was the biggest flirt in the whole company, chuckled to himself while she shoved her phone back into her side pocket and continued to restock her jump bag.

Paige McFarland didn't have time for personal relationships. She had more important things to do, like finish her facial recognition software and check in with her DCIS handler, Erik Rollands, who hadn't texted this morning like he normally did, asking her for updates.

Paige opened her mouth to retort back, but was interrupted by the radio. "Units two, three, and Rescue One. There is an MVC fifteen miles north on Highway 15. Two known victims. Male, fifty-eight, and female, fifty-five. Police on scene."

Paige grabbed her radio. "Unit two in route."

The one good thing about her partner, Marcus Newberg, was that he was one of the best EMTs in New Freedom. When they were on a call, he was the definition of a professional.

She would have to make contact with Rollands after they were done with this call. It wasn't like the computer program was magically going to fix itself. She just needed a few more days to get it perfect.

Marcus rushed down the highway as fast as the hairpin turns allowed him to go on this stretch of road.

Officer Harry Turvet was the officer on scene, and he waved them over about thirty yards away from where there was a hole in the guardrail.

The fire engine with rescue equipment was parked close to the scene. The crew was already setting up to go down the cliff. Paige placed her jump bag on the stretcher and waited for Marcus to help her unload it. She was the paramedic on duty and would need to be there when the victims, if they were alive, made it topside.

Peering over the cliff, she took in the details like her training had taught her to do. The car had hit a tree on the front passenger side. There was a broken branch jutting out of the windshield on the same side. What caught her eye, though, was the back bumper.

Someone had clearly hit this vehicle. She whipped her head back toward the road and took note of the tire marks. There were two sets. The first led directly towards the current car, but the second one indicated that the driver sped away from the accident. She logged that away and returned her focus to the firefighters working below.

Paige sucked in a sharp breath. She knew that car. Tears pricked the backs of her eyes. *Please don't let Rachel or any of the Craftons be seriously injured.* She and God were on shaky ground at best, but the plea fled her thoughts before she could stop it.

She could feel her heart rate accelerate and her vision hyper-focusing on the rescue in progress. Tucker Boykin's booming voice could be heard giving orders to the crew working in and around the car. He was their assistant chief and in charge of the rescue unit in New Freedom. The firefighters all respected him and expected him to be the next chief, which didn't happen. No one knew for sure whether he turned down the position or if he was never offered it.

The second ambulance pulled in behind them, and the other two EMTs on duty wheeled over their stretcher. All of their radios crackled to life with Tucker's command. "Topside, this is Rescue One, we have two victims. One female, fifty-five, BP 160/100, pulse eighty-five and strong, unconscious, head trauma with possible spine and neck injuries. One male, fifty-eight, conscious, bp 165/105, pulse one-twelve and thready, impalement to the right abdomen. We are sending him up first as soon as the impalement is stabilized."

"Rescue One, this is topside. We have two units standing by to transfer patients." Paige spoke with authority that came with her expertise in the field.

She rolled the stretcher closer to where two rescue crew members stood close to the wench. There were times in her military career that she would have had to make riskier climbs to reach a fellow soldier in need, but she was part of a team now. They were proficient at what they did. She just needed to be more patient.

The first basket with Mr. Crafton was carefully hoisted up the mountainside. They had him transferred to the stretcher in swift motions. Paige did her own visual assessment while Marcus and one of the rescue crew rolled him to the back of their rig. She placed her fingers on his wrist. His pulse was thready and racing. Climbing into the back with him, she began an IV and hooked him up to the monitors. She waved away the firefighter standing at the door.

"I've got this. Go help save his wife."

The firefighter gave her a curious look, but slammed the door shut and pounded on the back. As the unit pulled out, Charles grabbed her wrist with a firm grip, which surprised her, given his current state.

She patted his shoulder and kept putting on the heart leads. "We are on our way to the hospital. Just hang in there."

His raspy voice was barely a whisper. She had to lean closer to hear what he was saying. "The sparrow...has flown...help Rachel find her...she can stop this....you can trust Scott." Charles lifted his other hand and gave her a paper. "Eyes on Rachel."

Paige was confused. Who was the sparrow? And why would she need to trust Scott? Who was Scott? Was Rachel in trouble, too?

Before she could ask him anything, a high-pitched beep shut down her line of thinking and put her into full-on medic mode. Her one and only focus right now was keeping Charles Crafton alive. She could figure out what he meant after she got him to the hospital.

Alive.

On all of the missions to undisclosed places around the world, she had only lost two men in her care. She was not going to add to that number today.

Paige moved through the small space, fluidly placing the shock pads on his torso and turning on the machine. Beginning chest compressions, she willed the start-up to go faster as Marcus took a few of the turns a bit faster than she would have. Although his crazy driving would be for not if she couldn't get Charles' heart started again.

The calm voice on the defibrillator walked through the steps to restart the heart. Paige got the ambubag attached to the oxygen tank and began respirations in between the shocks. After two rounds of shock advised, Charles' heart restarted. Paige knew they weren't out of the woods yet. He had lost a lot of blood and needed to get to the hospital.

She placed the non-rebreather mask over his nose and checked the monitors for his heart rate and blood pressure. The firefighters on scene did an excellent job securing the impalement. She rechecked now that she had to do compressions.

They were only a few minutes out. She consulted with the hospital, giving them his vitals, injuries, sudden cardiac arrest—SCA—and their approximate arrival time. In that moment, she wanted to say another prayer, but God never listened to her prayers, so what was the point in wasting her mental space? She was the only one trying to keep Charles alive right now, and she needed to keep her focus.

Marcus made the sharp turn into the drive along the back side of the hospital towards the ambulance bay at the ER.

"Stay with me, Charles. We're here. Don't you die on me."

Charles didn't even flutter his eyes. He and his wife were good people. Who would want to run them off the road? Paige switched him to the portable tank of oxygen on the bottom of the stretcher and prepared to move him as soon as the doors opened.

Marcus threw the back doors open as ER staff greeted them. Paige gave the last set of vitals to Dr. Felton, the best ER doctor that New Freedom Hospital had. She was relieved to see he was the one on duty right now. Paige followed them past triage and into one of the private rooms. The team of nurses, doctors, and techs swarmed around her. They transferred him to the hospital gurney and hooked him up to their monitors. Paige moved the stretcher and portable equipment out of their way. As she exited the room, the steady beep of Charles' heart gave way to a screeching sound that had her own heart racing. Charles' heart had stopped again.

Chapter 2

"**G**OD, PLEASE, NOT CHARLES." Paige wanted to hit something or yell out in frustration. Why did the good people have to die? She knew her prayer wouldn't reach God's ears in time, but the words still slipped out of her mouth all the same. A team of people almost collided with her as they raced into the room with the crash cart. She stood staring at the room a moment longer, clenching and unclenching her fists.

Marcus stood in the hall waiting for her. "Let me get linens and restock the unit."

He thought that she needed a moment to deal with almost losing a patient. She would process that later. At home. Right now, she was going to take advantage of the moment alone and slip into an out-of-the-way spot so she could check out the paper Charles had given her. He said that it was "Eyes on Rachel". Looking at the numbers, she quickly realized that they were an IP address.

Paige jogged back to the rig and got her personal tablet out of her jump bag. The department gave them tough books for use on calls, but a computer nerd was hardly ever without some kind of their own tech.

She grabbed her encrypted hotspot and plugged it into her tablet. She designed the encryption code so that she could go just about anywhere and be able to connect to a network if she wanted to. She created her own virtual private network—VPN—pinging her IP address from one of thousands of servers across the world.

After using the biometrics scanner and inputting the password, Paige opened a web browser and entered the IP address. Twelve live camera feeds filled the screen. She saw her camper, which was parked on the back corner of the Craftons' land. How could she not have noticed the camera? She shook her head. Hopefully, Charles would pull through, and she could ask him about it later.

Movement on one of the other cameras caught her attention. She tapped the box, and the screen filled with that one live feed. A car sat down the dirt road from the end of the drive. Two men got out of the car with guns drawn. She recognized the one, Tylan Jamison. He was a PI who had his office in town. Rachel told her once that he was best friends with her brother before they both left for the military after high school. According to Rachel, he was cute, but way too intense for her.

Thinking about Rachel made Paige's heart squeeze. She hoped that her friend was safe. Paige closed the camera feed and returned to the home feed with all the cameras. She watched as Jamison and she assumed his partner, based on the way they communicated to one another without using words, made it through the woods. It's not like Paige could hear anything because the videos didn't have sound.

Booted footsteps approached from behind her. She closed out of the browser and shut down the tablet. If Rachel was at the cabin, she had every confidence that Jamison would be able to get to her and make sure she was safe.

"There you are." Paige turned to face Marcus. "I have some supplies to restock, but we are going to have to clean the back."

Paige winced. It was always harder when you knew the patient you were transporting. Cleaning up the blood of a friend, neighbor, or colleague was different than if it were a stranger. Not that she wouldn't try just as hard to save a stranger, but getting attached to someone and then seeing them fight for their life left a scar. This was why she didn't let people in. Because when she let them in and they got hurt, it destroyed a little bit more of her.

Marcus must have noticed Paige's hesitation because he offered to clean it for her. "Go sit in the waiting room. Maybe you can get an update from Trina. I'll sanitize the back and check in with you when I'm done." He paused. "Thought you would want to know... Mrs. Crafton is here but is still unconscious."

"Thanks," Paige croaked. The tears burned the backs of her eyes. She vowed to never shed a tear or to let people into her circle. She needed to get a hold of her emotions.

Paige cleared her throat. "I'll go see if Trina will give me an update on either one." She marched toward the ER's nurses' station. As she passed the room where she had left Mr. Crafton, it was empty. Her heart skipped a beat. She hoped that he was in surgery, not downstairs in the morgue.

The nurse's station was in a state of ever-moving coordinated chaos. Or at least that was what it always seemed to her. She spotted Trina Willet, the charge nurse for the Emergency Department—ED. Paige liked her. Trina was not someone you would want to mess with on the best of days, and today looked like she was on a warpath.

"If you are about to ask me to break confidentiality laws and give you information on someone not related to you, you can keep on walking." Trina's dark curls were pulled back into a high ponytail, showing off her strong jaw and exposing her fierce eyes, giving her a warrior vibe. She stared at Paige, daring her to ask.

Paige matched her piercing gaze with one of her own. "I'm checking on the patient that I just brought in here." Without giving her an opportunity to cut her off, Paige continued. "Charles Crafton. The one with the tree branch sticking out of his abdomen."

Trina's nostrils flared, and her eyes flashed with fire for a brief moment before that was replaced by compassion. "They were able to get his heart started and stabilized enough that they just wheeled him into surgery. And that's all I'm saying."

Paige knew that she wasn't going to get anything else out of Trina about Mr. Crafton. "I'm going to wait in the waiting room. His daughter is my friend, and I want to be here for her when she comes in."

If she comes in. Paige wanted to stay positive, but between the skid marks on the road, Charles' cryptic message, and the security cameras on their property, she wasn't sure what to believe about the generous couple.

Paige found a quiet corner in the waiting area away from everyone else. She pulled out her phone and tried texting Rachel. She would give her a few minutes to respond. Rachel preferred to text instead of talking on the phone.

Paige bounced the phone on her leg a few times and then decided to open the camera footage on her tablet again. She searched the boxes to see if she could find Jamison or his partner. The front door opened and Jamison came out with Rachel between him and his partner as if they were protecting her. Rachel was looking around and asked Tylan something. Tylan talked over his shoulder but kept his eyes searching everything around them. He spotted the camera and said something to Rachel. Rachel shrugged and responded. Why hadn't Charles gotten cameras with audio capabilities?

Paige watched as the trio kept to the tree line and made their way back to the car. Well, at least Rachel was safe. She hoped that she was coming here. If Rachel knew what happened, she wouldn't want to be anywhere else.

Clicking out of the single view, Paige noticed that there were a few cameras at the Craftons' house. Two covering the front door and east side of the house and two covering the opposite corner, as well as one covering the front and side of the garage. If she remembered correctly, they also had one of those camera doorbells, although she didn't see that feed here. She clicked on the camera facing the front of their house and noticed the front door was cracked open.

She took a screenshot of the door and opened a photo editing software she kept on her tablet. She zoomed in and focused the picture. Through the window and opening of the door she saw a shattered lamp, the one that used to sit on the table just inside their door.

She needed to report this to the police, but how was she going to explain how she knew to go to their house? Maybe she could text Rachel and ask her to tell the police.

At that moment, Marcus walked into the space with his arm around a young nurse, Kelli, according to her name tag. Paige put her tablet to sleep and grabbed her tough book.

"There you are, partner." Marcus said, sweet as honey. Despite his charm, Paige would never fall for him. He wasn't her type. He was overconfident, flashy, and thought too highly of himself. Unfortunately, Kelli bought his act hook, line, and sinker by the way she was staring at him.

"Do you mind if I finish up the paperwork and we wait here for our next call?" Paige knew it wasn't technically against protocol, but it wasn't normal behavior either.

Marcus only hesitated briefly before turning to Kelli. "Would you mind doing our coffee date now at the cafe instead of tomorrow?"

Kelli beamed at him. "Of course."

"We'll be down the hall in the food court." Marcus lifted his chin.

"I'll mind the radio. Enjoy your date."

Once they were down the hall, Paige got to work on finishing her report and sending it off. As Paige radioed in that they were clear of the call, Rachel came bursting through the doors, followed by Jamison and his partner. Paige thought she recognized him from somewhere, but she couldn't place his name.

Rachel walked straight to the nurses' station and barked at Trina, "My parents were in a car crash and were taken here. Give me an updated status on them."

Trina blinked at Rachel a moment before sitting and asking, "What are their names?"

"Charles and Paola Crafton." Rachel came off sometimes as cold, but Paige knew she felt deeply.

Paige stood and made her way towards Rachel. Her movement caught the attention of Tylan and his partner. They shifted to be between Paige and Rachel, but not before Paige made eye contact with her.

"Paige, can you help me find out what is taking so long to be given the status of my parents?" Rachel blurted.

The fire returned to Trina's eyes and Paige fought a smile. Rachel was brilliant, but sometimes she did not understand why people did not process things as quickly as she did.

Paige stepped past Tylan and faced Trina. "You can understand that she is worried about her parents. We will take an update whenever you have it."

Paige's placating words seemed to extinguish the flames of her anger because Trina put on her best customer service smile and said, "Of course. Mr. Crafton is still in surgery and Mrs. Crafton is in a CT scan right now. I will let the doctors know you are here and they will come out with an update when they have one. You can sit over there while you wait." She pointed to the area where Paige had been sitting.

"Thank you." Paige steered Rachel away before her friend could say anything else.

"I don't know what her problem was. I was just asking about my parents."

"I know, Rachel."

Once they reached the seat she had occupied before, Paige faced Jamison and extended her hand. "I'm Paige MacFarland. And you are?"

"I'm Tylan Jamison and this is my partner, Ronnie Dupont." He handed her a business card identifying himself as the PI from in town. "We are friends of the family."

Interesting that he did not mention searching the Craftons' property with guns or protecting Rachel even though their behaviors at the nurses' station screamed bodyguards.

"Well, it's nice to meet you, Tylan. Ronnie. I can sit here with Rachel if you need to go do some PI things." She waved the business card between her two fingers.

Tylan's sharp dark eyes narrowed slightly. "I think we will stay too, if you don't mind. It looks like you are on duty. We wouldn't want Rachel to be alone in this hard time."

Rachel snorted. "Just tell her Scott sent you to protect me because he is freaking out about nothing. You know I'm perfectly capable of taking care of myself. I'm not twelve anymore."

Scott. Charles said to trust him. Scott must be their son that Paola talked about. The one fighting wildfires or something like that. She hoped she guessed right.

"I'm sure your brother only wants to keep you safe. When was the last time you talked with him?" Paige leaned close to Rachel so that Tylan couldn't hear. "Maybe he would call off the guards if he knew you were fine."

"I doubt it." Rachel sat with a huff and put her head in her hands.

Tylan excused himself. Probably had to check in with a client wanting answers.

Ronnie leaned his shoulder against the wall and spoke for the first time. "So, Paige, besides volunteering as an EMT, what do you do for work?"

"What Paige does for a living or in her free time is of no concern to you," Rachel snapped. "My father trusts her. Otherwise, she wouldn't be living on our property under his protection."

Paige whipped her head to face Rachel. "Rachel what are you talking about 'under his protection'? What exactly does your dad do? I thought he was retired."

Rachel shrugged her one shoulder. "He is retired. Sorta."

This day kept turning upside down. Paige knew she should process everything, but she didn't want to do that in front of the PI.

"Well, that is as clear as the morning fog in the Smokies," she said instead.

"Sorry. I am not allowed to say anything in an insecure location," Rachel responded curtly.

Paige considered her answer and decided to change the subject. Now that Rachel was here, maybe she could show her the camera feeds and they could take care of the intruder.

"Can I show you something? I was the one that brought your dad in. He gave me this." Paige handed her the paper with the IP address on it.

"Not surprised that he gave you that. He thinks of you as another daughter." Rachel's shoulders relaxed a bit. "It has been nice having a sister. People don't get me, but you do."

Ronnie took a step forward to see what was on the paper, but Rachel crumpled it up and stuck it in her pocket. "Do you have a tablet or computer with your VPN hotspot?" she asked.

"Would I ever be without one?" Paige asked sarcastically.

"I've never seen you without one, but I thought I would be nice and ask."

Paige laughed. "I was only joking."

Rachel squeaked then snorted a laugh. "Good one."

Ronnie stared at them, confused at the exchange. He shook his head and went back to leaning against the wall, ever watching the room.

Paige unlocked her tablet and handed it to Rachel. Rachel launched the cameras and then started typing in code, which brought up the recorded history of the feeds.

"Ronnie, you and Tylan look professional. Good job."

Ronnie was confused by her statement and looked over her shoulder at the tablet. Clarity slid across his face as their whole conversation now made more sense.

"Thanks. Let me know if you have any footage of people lurking around. Do you have cameras at the house?"

Rachel tapped the screens a few times and sucked in a breath. "Ronnie, I need your phone."

"You don't have yours?" He lifted his eyebrows at her.

Rachel narrowed her eyes, "You guys told me that my parents were in a car crash and my pack with everything in it was in the bunker. Safe. Now give me a phone. Please."

Bunker? What bunker? Who were these people? Questions raced through Paige's mind.

Rachel took Ronnie's phone and dialed 911. "This is Rachel Crafton. I would like to report a break in at 23 Blackbird Lane." Rachel paused, listening. "I am not there, but I am looking at the security feed." Another pause. "I am at the hospital. My parents were in a car accident, which was probably not an accident given that their place was broken into. You may send the police to the hospital and I will give them a recording of the security cameras. Thank you." Rachel hung up and handed Ronnie his phone back.

"Your parents' house was broken into?" he asked.

Rachel turned the tablet so that he could see the zoomed in view of the front door showing a piece of the destruction inside.

"What these guys lack in intelligence they probably make up for in strength." Paige and Ronnie stared at Rachel. She sighed, "Dad would never keep anything secure at the house. He wanted to protect Mom and me from that."

"We'll circle back to that when we aren't here," Paige began. "But first, tell me how I am under your dad's protection."

"Rollands and Dad go way back. When you proclaimed you were going to take your camper and find a spot to get away from the crazy to work alone, Rollands contacted my dad to make sure you stayed safe. Dad figured the easiest way to do that was to allow you to camp on our property. After you were vetted, of course."

"Huh and ouch."

"Are you hurt?"

"Only my pride. I thought I was good at reading people. How could I miss all of this?"

"Don't let it bother you." Rachel waved her hand in the air. "Mom says that Dad is one of the best at what he does. It's how they met, but that's another story for another time."

Paige looked at Ronnie, who looked like he had as many questions as she did about this whole thing.

"You can tell me all about it when I get off my shift in the morning." Paige reclined further into the char. "I'll stay until I get another call."

"Thanks, Paige."

Chapter 3

S COTT WAS PUTTING AS much distance behind him as he could without getting caught for breaking the speed limit. He should be to New Freedom in about twenty minutes. For the last hour and fifteen minutes, Scott had turned over his mother's words and sent more prayers heavenward. He was going to need God in order to get through this.

Who was he protecting Rachel from, exactly? Had his parents' past finally caught up with them? Scott gripped the steering wheel until his knuckles were white.

"God, whatever is going on, please protect Rachel." She was someone else he needed to ask forgiveness from. When he left after high school, determined to prove himself, he also left her. She was quite possibly the smartest person he had ever known, but being on the spectrum meant that she missed social cues. Things like sarcasm were lost on her.

He remembered the morning he left for basic.

"You're not coming back, are you?" Rachel looked at him with her eyebrows pulled together slightly.

"When it's over, I'll be back."

She probably thought he meant when basic was over, but he was thinking along the lines of this standoff with his father.

Scott shook his head. He was such a hot head and blinded by guilt. Most days he had let the guilt go, but he still had bad days where the doubt and guilt roared to life inside.

He should have heard from Tylan by now. He didn't want to call in case they were in a situation where radio silence was necessary.

Just then, ringing came through the speakers of his truck. Tylan. "Give me the sitrep."

"Rachel is safe. We are here at the hospital. She wanted to come here as soon as she heard about your parents."

Scott blew out a breath. "Tell me what happened."

"I brought Ronnie Dupont with me. He started working with me a few months ago. I trust him, but he does not know about your parents' past or present work."

Scott thought that his dad would have retired completely by now and his mother hadn't worked since Rachel was born. Something else he would have to talk with him about. If he survived.

Scott pushed those thoughts aside. "We approached the cabin from the road." Tylan kept going. "There was no sign of forced entry. I went around back and Ronnie took the front. Once he breached the front door, Rachel shot over his head."

"Wait. My sister knows how to use a gun?" She hated the sound it made. Or at least she had.

"You've been gone a long time, Scott. People change. Rachel has grown into a fierce, brilliant young woman. No one who actually knows her would go up against her."

What? Scott shook his head as the guilt of leaving started to settle in again. What if his father groomed her to follow in the family legacy like he wanted Scott to do? He only prayed that she was not put through the same training he had been.

"Before you blame yourself for leaving her behind, your father refused to train her." Tylan also knew how to read his mind. Some things hadn't changed at least. "He was protective of her, given her intelligence level. When I returned home, she was seventeen and helping your mom run the self-defense classes at the gym. I asked her where she learned her moves and she told me that her father refused to teach her. So, she signed up to take the self-defense class, only to find it was her mom as the instructor. She made me promise not to tell her dad. She was going to tell him when she turned eighteen. I've always wondered how that conversation went."

"She's going to be upset that I sent you to protect her, isn't she?"

"You could say that," Tylan deadpanned.

"So what happened after she shot at Ronnie?"

"She demanded Ronnie identify himself and said she wouldn't miss next time if she didn't like his answer. Thankfully he remembered the safe code and she stood down." Tylan barked a laugh. "You should have seen his face. He was both surprised and impressed."

29

"Well, I guess I've got some catching up to do. Is she with you right now?"

"Right now she is sitting with Paige MacFarland, a volunteer paramedic. She is good with Rachel and Rachel seems to trust her. I think she might be the one Charles was telling me about. Something about a computer programmer needing a quiet place to complete their work, but she is not what I would call your typical computer geek."

Scott wasn't sure what that meant. "Can she be trusted?"

"I can run a profile on her if you want me to."

Scott didn't want to snoop into someone else's past for no good reason. He knew what it was like to carry secrets that he wanted no one else to know. He sighed. "Do *you* think she can be trusted?"

"Yes. Charles wouldn't let her get close to Rachel if he didn't trust her."

"That's good enough for me. Thanks, Tylan."

They disconnected and the silence in the truck afterward almost sent Scott into a tailspin. His baby sister was not only grown, but by the sounds of it, was as deadly with her brain as her aim. His mom was right, New Freedom wasn't the same. Or at least, not his sister.

He wasn't the same boy who had left either. The air force molded the stubbornness that drove him to leave into a decorated fighter pilot. He had wanted to make something of himself, given the failure he was when he left. He prayed that, on his return home, he could prove that he was someone that people could trust.

Scott finally made it to the hospital and strode in the door. Rachel was sitting next to a woman with pixie cut hair and a mop of red curls on the top of her head. She was in the town's volunteer EMS uniform which only hid her curves slightly. Rising to her full height, she stood in front of Rachel with her hands on her hips. Those emerald eyes held a keen determination as she took in his presence. When they stopped at his face, he could have sworn that he saw a slight lift of the corner of her mouth.

"You must be Scott," the fiery redhead said. "You look like a younger version of your dad."

Rachel stood and rolled her eyes. "Paige, this is Scott. Scott, this is Paige. Now that you know each other, you both can stop acting like I'm incapable of defending myself. Scott, you owe me a hug."

Rachel had turned into a younger version of their mother. Trim. Tall. Long auburn hair up in a high ponytail, but her eyes were just like his and Dad's—blue with a hint of gray around the outside.

"It's good to see you, kid." He gave her a hug.

"You can stop calling me a kid," she squeaked as she tightened the embrace. She pushed back. "If you haven't noticed, I've grown up since you never came back."

Ouch. Yep, she still didn't pull any punches.

"I deserved that one." Scott rubbed his neck, "I'm back now, and well..." What did he say after twelve years of absence? Out of the corner of his eye, he saw Paige shift as if this was the most awkward reunion she had been a part of.

"Promise not to leave again when stuff happens, because I don't think I can stand it again if you abandon me."

Rachel's blunt words were like a kick to the solar plexus. "I've done some growing up too since I've been gone."

"Mom told me." Rachel narrowed her eyes at him. She really was a different person. The Rachel he knew hated conflict; it exasperated her anxiety. This woman before him was fierce, to use Tylan's words.

"Where's Tylan?"

"His daughter, Sari, is home from daycare sick. He is talking with his mom, Jean, to see how they are." Rachel accented Sari's name as if Scott needed a lesson on who was who. One of the many good things about talking with his mom between missions was that he was current, or at least as current as last week, on the town happenings. "You know he was married, right? To Fahta, and that your predecessor was the one to kill her?"

Paige winced.

"I'm aware." Scott cleared his throat. "I was training that weekend and couldn't make the wedding, but I sent them a gift. And Mom said he didn't have a public funeral for her, or I would have made every effort to be there." He was rambling.

Rachel snorted. "Some best friend."

Scott opened his mouth to retort about duty, but Paige beat him to it. "Rachel, you know how the government works. You don't really get a say in when you get time off. I'm sure if he was on leave, he would have been there."

Paige spoke like someone who knew of this firsthand. He would have to ask about that later.

"You're right," Rachel huffed.

Scott could see that he would have his work cut out for him in terms of making up for his absence to Rachel. He had hurt her deeply, something he had no intention of doing in the first place. Coming back was going to be rough, he knew that the moment he took the fire chief position, but facing it with his own sister almost took it out of him. He needed to do something. He paced over to the nurses station to see if he could get an update on his parents.

A doctor walked into the waiting room. "The family of Paola Crafton?"

Rachel strode toward the man. "Here." She pointed to Scott too. He would take the acknowledgement. It was a start.

"I'm Dr. Felton. She is still in a coma and has suffered a concussion. We will be admitting and monitoring her. We won't know if there is any brain damage until she wakes up."

Scott absorbed the doctor's words but felt numb. He knew he was slipping into professional mode, but he could process this later. When he was alone.

"Could we see her before you move her to her room?" Dr. Felton hesitated. Scott added, "Please, we will only be a moment and if they come to get her, we will leave. Promise."

Dr. Felton nodded. "I guess that will be fine. Just to warn you, she has lacerations across her face and a broken clavicle from the impact of the seat belt. The cuts are mostly superficial, but she has bandages for the deeper ones and has her arm immobilized."

Scott nodded and allowed Rachel to go first. He looked back at Paige. She gave him a slight nod and took a seat. Good, Rachel would need a friend, someone she trusted, to help her through this.

Scott followed Rachel through the private room in the back of the ER. The steady beat of the heart monitor told him that Mom was alive, but she seemed so still. Rachel went on the far side of the bed. She pulled up a chair and rested her head on her mother's arm. The side closest to the door where Scott stood was filled with IV poles and the heart monitor. Seeing no other room, Scott placed his hand on her leg.

"Hey Mom," he squeezed past the rock in his throat. "I made it. Rachel is safe. We'll find out what happened."

Scott looked at his sister as she lifted her head at his statement. She gave him a curt nod. "We promise," she added.

The door to the room opened and a man and woman wearing matching scrubs with the words *Patient Transport* scrolled across the left chest pushed in a gurney.

"I'm sorry, but we are here to take her to her room." The woman spoke with authority. "You'll have to wait out in the lobby. A nurse will tell you where you can meet us. Give us about fifteen to twenty minutes to get her upstairs and situated."

Having been dismissed, Scott and Rachel made their way out to the front station where Trina sat at her computer. Trina was about ten years older than Scott, but her youngest brother was only a grade ahead of him in school. He was hoping she didn't remember who he was back then or why he left.

"Well, look who decided to finally come back home." Trina crossed her arms. "Scott Crafton. Jonell will be happy to see you again." She relaxed her arms and smiled at him. That was a better reception than he was expecting.

"Thanks, Trina."

She looked past him to Rachel and back to him. "I see it now. It's in your eyes. What can I do for you?"

"Do you know what room they are taking Paola Crafton to?"

Trina typed quickly and wrote down a number on a piece of paper. When she handed it to him, she didn't release it right away. "I'm glad you took the fire chief position. This town needs someone they can trust."

Scott held her gaze a moment longer before she let go. He hoped that he could live up to that trust. He wasn't the same boy that had left. Only time would tell if more people had Trina's attitude of acceptance or if they still blamed him for what happened.

He wanted to thank Paige again for waiting with Rachel until he got here. She put up a hand in a stopping motion before he said a word.

"Rachel is my friend and so are your parents. I told her that I would come back as soon as my shift is over in the morning." She gathered her jump bag from the chair. "We just got a call. I've got to go save a young nurse from the charms of my partner."

She started walking towards the hall that led to the food court. When she reached the hall, she turned back. "And, Chief, welcome back to New Freedom. See you at the station."

Her smile made his heart tick up a few beats. Scott mentally chided himself. He was her superior; there was no way that he could have feelings for someone in his company. A friendship at most, and even that he would have to be careful not to show any favorites or special treatments.

She intrigued him, though. She carried herself with confidence, which immediately demanded respect, but she wasn't full of herself like some paramedics he knew. Clearly, she could read people well because she knew what he was going to say before he said a word. That was something he wanted in the paramedics under his charge. He felt his lips curl as he watched her disappear.

"It'll never work, so stop daydreaming." His sister's words slapped him out of his thoughts.

"It's not like that. I'm just thankful I have someone so competent in the company." He looked Rachel in the eyes. "And clearly a good friend of my sister's."

"Whatever you say, Griz." The old moniker that she had called him sprouted hope in his heart. Just maybe she would forgive him.

"Let's go see if Mom is settled yet," he said as he walked away.

Scott and Rachel made it to the fourth floor ICU where their mother would be kept until she woke up and they could evaluate her injuries more. For now she had a nonrebreather mask over her nose and mouth, but did not need a ventilator. He would count that as a victory. It was hard to see his mom like this. She was always so strong like nothing phased her.

Rachel sat down next to the bed and started telling Mom about how she almost shot Ronnie.

"You should have seen his face, Mom. I missed on purpose like you taught me, but he jumped, then ducked before shouting the safe phrase."

Scott watched his sister. She certainly was not the same little girl he left all those years ago. He was trying to wrap his brain around his mom being the one to teach Rachel how to shoot and, apparently, how to defend herself. In his mind, his father was the one who brought the dangerous past into the family, but maybe he should ask similar questions about his mother.

The longer he stayed here the more questions he had. He needed to do something about it. As fire chief, he would have access to the emergency logs and know who the responding officer was on the scene. He'd start there because the urge to move, to do something, could not be contained any longer.

Scott paced toward the door. "I'm going to see what I can find out about the accident. Call me when she wakes up?"

Rachel narrowed her eyes, but said nothing. Instead she gave him a curt nod.

"I'll have either Ronnie or Tylan stay with you." He put his hand up to stop her protest. "It's for my peace of mind. It's clear you can defend yourself."

He watched the fight simmer out in her eyes. "Fine. Keep me in the loop?"

"Of course."

Scott paced through the door to find Ronnie talking to a woman who had her back to him. "I'm sorry to interrupt, but could you stay close? I'm going to go talk with the officer on scene..."

The rest of his words died on his lips as the woman turned around. Dayton Zeits. Just like that, the past hit him like a train. If anyone in the world had a right to never forgive him or trust him, it was Dayton.

Ronnie shifted and placed an arm around Dayton. "I'm sure you remember Dayton. She and I have been married for eight years." The two looked at each other and Scott would have had to have been a blind man to miss the connection that they shared.

Dayton stuck out her hand, "It's good to see you again, Scott." They shook hands. "I'm glad you came back. We have to face our demons if we ever want to be free."

"Easier said than done," he grunted.

He could worry about dealing with the past later. Right now, he needed to know what happened to his parents.

Ronnie clamped him on the shoulder. "Tylan and I will take turns standing watch, but if Rachel leaves, I'm going to stay with your mom. I have experienced how well Rachel can defend herself, but your mom isn't conscious."

Ronnie had a valid point. Scott gave a nod. "Thanks. Call if anything happens. It was good to see you again, Dayton."

He wouldn't classify it as good to see her, but the past wasn't her fault. Maybe returning to New Freedom wouldn't be as difficult as he thought it would be...as soon as he could figure out what was going on with his own family.

Chapter 4

W HAT IN THE WORLD was wrong with her?

Relationships only leave you with a heartache. She was perfectly fine being alone. It's the whole reason she came out to this small mountain town anyway.

DC had too many people, all with their own agenda. If she was honest with herself, she was starting to enjoy being a part of the fire company again, and the Craftons were people that she trusted.

Although, she wasn't sure how she felt about Rollands asking Charles to protect her. She was perfectly capable of that herself. Hank made sure of that. The thought of him made the pain rattle the cage she kept it in. Pushing the seams, wanting out so that it could control her again.

Paige blinked away the tears that were threatening to come. She needed to focus on the job; she could daydream about handsome fire chiefs and avoid dealing with the past later. She snorted at herself for even wanting to daydream about any man.

"What's so funny?" Marcus asked without taking his eyes off the road.

"Nothing. I'm just a funny person in my head."

Marcus gave her a bemused smile. "Whatever you say."

She wanted to punch him in the arm. "You're lucky you're driving."

That got Marcus to laugh.

"See? I am a funny person."

They came to the assisted living and retirement complex just outside of town. Ms. Betty Miller was the town's beloved kindergarten teacher who taught until she could no longer physically handle the long days at the age of seventy-five. Never having been married or children of her own, she loved every child that stepped foot in her class as if they were her own.

She was now a frequent flier for New Freedom EMS, at least overnight when the nursing staff for the independent living section of the complex was not there.

After they checked her out and bandaged her cut on her arm that she got when she fell, Paige cleaned up her supplies.

"Ms. Betty, you need to be careful or you'll never get out of here," Marcus joked.

Betty laughed that grandmotherly laugh of hers. "Oh, child, I'm not getting out of here. In fact, I've already talked with Stanley Fox about selling my place. This apartment is expensive and I need all the money I can get if I plan to be here a while." Betty looked around the tidy, single bedroom apartment. It was just enough space for one person.

Stanley Fox was the town's golden boy who could do no wrong in the eyes of so many people. To Paige, he seemed to be slicker than a used car salesman pawning off lemons. There was something in his eyes that most people mistook with sincerity, but Paige saw it as calculated manipulation. It was probably due to too many years seeing the worst side of humanity.

"What is it, child?" Ms. Betty asked her.

"Nothing. You be careful now." Paige gave the elderly woman a pat on her hand and headed out with Marcus.

Once they made it to the safety of their unit, Marcus looked at her. "Where to, boss?"

Paige rolled her eyes. "Let's go back to the station. I'll finish the paperwork on the way."

They were almost back to the station by the time she finished her report. Marcus kept stealing glances at her as if he wanted to ask her something.

"You going to ask me your question or just continue staring?" Paige didn't like playing games. That's why she loved being around Rachel so much. Rachel pulled no punches, but you never had to guess what she actually meant.

Marcus stopped in the driveway and faced her. "You don't like Stanley Fox? The town's hero?"

Town hero was a stretch. He was the one that called 911 when his father slammed into Fahta Jamison. Which, in her book, hardly qualified him as a hero. He also bought a whole block of vacant buildings in town, tore them all down and donated the block to the town as a playground for the children. That might get him good guy status, but hero? Not even close.

"Let's just say he's not my type."

Marcus smirked as he backed the unit into the bay, "What is your type?"

"None of your business." Paige waved him off. "Why don't you save your antics for someone who enjoys your charms."

Paige hopped out and went to work checking and re-stocking what they needed while Marcus made his way to the living quarters and something that smelled delicious. When she finished in the bay she set out looking for the source of the tantalizing food. Walking down the hallway towards the living quarters and kitchen, she saw a light on in the chief's office. As she approached, voices floated toward her through the cracked door.

Tucker's booming voice filled the space. "When we got there, Officer Turvet was securing the area."

Paige stopped beside the door to hear who Tucker was talking with and where the conversation was going. She just hoped that no one came this way and caught her snooping.

"Did you notice anything odd at the scene?" Scott's baritone voice made her heart tick up a notch. Stupid heart. She would have to work hard to get it under control.

"I noticed two sets of skid marks as if the car was run off the road. Besides, there was no rain or other reason to believe that it would have been driver error."

She took note of how both men's voices were deep and rich. They both demanded respect when they walked into the room. If Scott could earn the trust of Tucker, she had no doubt that the whole company would rally behind their new chief. Only time would tell.

"I see here that Bryson went along for coverage with my mother, but no one is listed as an assistant to my father. Just Paige. Wait. Paige was the one who took care of my dad?" Papers wrestled. "Isn't it SOP to have a partner in the back especially for trauma patients? Did you not have people to spare?"

Paige felt her blood pressure starting to rise. She was perfectly capable of treating any patient on her own. No one was there when the unit she was embedded with was ambushed. She was starting to like the company of the fire station, but she didn't need help. Paige breathed slowly, needing to hear Tucker's response.

"Paige is one of the most gifted paramedics that I've ever met." Tucker paused. "Her only fault that I can see is that she is a bit of a lone wolf. She is so good at what she does that she views any assistance as unnecessary."

Tucker's words were like a slap to her face. They were her exact thoughts, but coming from someone whose leadership and opinion she had come to admire, they stung.

Then Scott asked the question surfacing in her brain. "What if my father would have died because she refused to have an extra set of hands to help her? It's not a question of doubting her skill, it's as simple as two sets of skilled hands get the work done quicker and in critical situations, seconds matter."

Logic and her pride warred for space in her thoughts. Anger wanted to hold its ground and continue to color her view, but Scott's words broke through. *'It's not a question of doubting her skill'.* She wanted to believe the tall, fit fire chief with the short-cropped sandy-blond hair and gray-blue eyes. Unless he commanded her to take someone with her, she would continue to save people on her own.

She was better off alone.

Movement down the hall made Paige take a step away from the wall so she wouldn't be caught eavesdropping.

Marcus called out to her. "Paige, you should get some of Bryson's stew before it's all gone. Don't know what the night will hold for us."

Without looking at the office, Paige took a step towards Marcus and the kitchen. "You know you're going to regret saying that."

She didn't necessarily believe in superstitions, but it seemed that when someone wished for a quiet night or to just get solid sleep, they were running all night. Marcus gave her a face of mock horror before breaking into laughter.

"Come on, partner, lighten up. We've already had our excitement for the day."

The sound of the alarm system interrupted her retort. Paige and Marcus ran down the hallway, checking the screen next to the entrance of the bay. It was a house fire and her unit was put on standby as support for the fire crew. The address seemed familiar, but she couldn't place who owned it.

Marcus gave a frustrated grunt. "That's Ms. Betty's place."

Paige and Marcus were in their unit and ready to pull out when she glanced over to the fire chief's truck as Scott climbed into the driver seat with full turnout gear thrown in the passenger seat. They all would find out what Scott was like as a chief sooner than they thought.

Marcus cruised down Main Street, past store fronts whose shops had closed hours ago, towards the oldest neighborhood in New Freedom. It was a quaint neighborhood filled with cookie-cutter houses circa 1960's with one main road, Oak Drive, that had side roads labeled with other arborous names ending in cul-de-sacs.

As the engine in front of them turned onto Oak Drive, Molly Bryant's voice came across the radio. "We have a two story wood-frame at 1324 Willow Avenue. Smoke showing from the Charlie Delta corner of the structure. Windows darkened. No flames visible from the outside. Waiting for engine to proceed."

Molly worked for her father's mechanic shop in town and volunteered when her ex-husband had the kids. She said it kept her mind off of the empty house. Try as she may, Paige resisted Molly's attempts at friendship. It wasn't that Molly wasn't nice or anything, but it seemed that drama followed her like a lost puppy and Paige moved here to have peace. Not drama.

Turning onto Willow Avenue, Marcus turned the ambulance around and parked along the street just outside the cul-de-sac. Ms. Miller's house was the one at the top with its back yard up against the forested area beyond the neighborhood.

Thick, dark smoke pushed and poured from the back corner of the house. Paige was not a firefighter, but she had been to many fires as a paramedic. The thick, dark smoke indicated that the fire was starved for oxygen. If they were to breach by opening a door or window, oxygen would rush in, feeding and spreading the fire toward the new air.

Tucker and his truck crew poured from their engine with practiced precision. Each member grabbed the gear they needed for their assigned task. Kent Bryson, the engine driver, grabbed his halligan and the first ground ladder. Scott joined him as they made their way toward the house. Bryson looked for gas to the house that may need to be turned off while Scott took in the structure as a whole, looking for points of entry, reading the smoke, and making a plan of action that would hopefully keep everyone safe.

Tucker gave instructions to Molly and Mateo Cruz, a relatively new recruit fresh out of high school. The two grabbed the specified hose and started to lay the first line to the house as Scott rounded the corner. He approached Tucker. What Paige wouldn't give to be able to hear their conversation. She wanted to respect Crafton as the chief, but she was still wrestling with what she overheard in his office. She saved his father. He should be thankful, not criticizing her work.

All she could do for now was stand off to the side with her jump bag and hope that they didn't need her. The urge to pray for each of the firefighters' safety was strong, but she shoved it away. She had prayed every mission and that hadn't stopped those she cared about from dying. Scott was the one that would keep them all as safe as possible. They would have to rely on him.

Scott's voice cracked through the radio, "Cruz and Bryant, cut a vent towards the Delta side. Boykin and Jones, you are on search."

Tucker, holding the thermal imaging camera, TIC, and hook slung over his shoulder, approached the front door with Kevin Jones carrying the pressurized water, PW can. They waited until Cruz and Bryant radioed that the vent was in place before breaching the door and making their search for anyone.

Paige watched Scott. He listened and observed every part of the scene. His keen eyes took in every detail. He and the crew moved in sync, like they'd spent years honing their skills side by side. Watching the new chief read the fire and stay a step ahead of his crew's needs, Paige couldn't help but be impressed. She might even be able to respect his criticism of her actions. One day.

"All quadrants clear on the first floor," Tucker reported across the radio. "Fire contained to the Charlie Delta corner of the structure on this floor."

Scott gave orders to the engine that had just arrived. They would start laying lines and suppressing the fire. Paige waited on edge while Tucker and Jones continued to clear the house. She knew that Ms. Miller was safe in her apartment, but when a house sat empty like this, some people tried to use it for themselves.

As the fire seemed to be coming under control, Paige heard a call she dreaded.

"Man down. Mechanism of injury unknown. Cruz is unresponsive, but breathing." Molly's voice came through the radio. "Need EMS."

Paige grabbed her jump bag and portable oxygen tank while Marcus carried the backboard. They wouldn't get too close to the structure for fear of being in the way, but they would meet Molly on the grass so she did not have to drag Cruz too far.

Molly emerged from the house moments later with Cruz clipped to her harness. Marcus held on to his torso while Molly unhooked him. Paige worked with her to remove his helmet, turnout jacket, and self-contained breathing tank while Marcus removed his breathing apparatus mask.

They gently laid him on the back board and Paige began to evaluate him, starting with his head. While she checked for obvious outward injuries, Marcus took his blood pressure, pulse, oxygen saturation, and respirations. Molly shed her turnout jacket and SCBA gear.

"Help me take off the turnout pants," Paige addressed Molly. "Then clean and dress the wound on his left temporal region."

She wasn't sure how he sustained that injury given the helmet that he was wearing. Something to worry about later. They worked together to remove his turnout pants so that Paige could finish her injury inventory.

"What happened to you, Cruz?" Paige whispered.

Satisfied that there were no other obvious outward injuries, and with his blood pressure and heart rate within normal range, Paige strapped Cruz to the backboard so that they could carry him to the stretcher waiting on the sidewalk while Marcus adjusted a non-rebreather over the young firefighter's face. Scott momentarily left his post to help them lift Cruz.

Paige filled him in. "He has a laceration to the left temporal region. His blood pressure and heart rate are stable."

Swiftly and efficiently they transferred him from the back board to the stretcher. Scott grabbed a hold of her arm before they could push Cruz away.

"Take Bryant with you." He put his hand up to stop her protest. "It has nothing to do with your skills and everything to do with keeping everyone safe." He stared her hard in the eyes, showing deep knowledge and concern. "It is better to have assistance and not need any than to need some and be all alone."

All the arguments bubbling within her died at his words. She gave him a curt nod.

"Molly, you're with me in the back. Let's move."

The shock on Molly's face disappeared as quickly as it came. *See, I can follow orders just like a good soldier.*

Paige was surprised at how well the two of them worked together. When Cruz started to wake up, Molly was the one who was able to calm him down. Mateo's dramatic start back to reality had Paige even more curious as to what actually happened in that house.

Once they got Mateo to the hospital and into the capable hands of the ED, all of the questions Paige had came flooding back. How could Mateo be hit if he was wearing his helmet? Did one of the other firefighters see anything?

Where was Molly? She was his partner at the moment and the one that found him.

What about the Craftons? Surely these two things weren't related, but it was another mystery that just didn't add up. Who would want to hurt them? She pondered about each of the incidents from the day while she cleaned and put the ambulance back into order.

When she came back into the ER waiting room for the second time in less than twenty four hours, Paige saw that Trina had gone home for the day and an older woman with salt-and-pepper hair pulled back into a tight bun sat in her spot. The woman looked like a well-trained guard with dark eyes and not even a hint of a smile on her face. Paige wished that Trina would have still been here. She may have been able to get something from her. Paige shook her head slightly; probably not.

She bypassed the nurses station and sat next to Molly. The smells of antiseptic mixed together with the smoke that rolled off of Molly was a unique combination that turned her stomach.

Molly had her elbows on her knees with her face in her hands. Exhaustion. Adrenaline crash. Worry. They all oozed from her.

At the sound of Paige sitting next to her, Molly ran her fingers through her hair and dropped her hands to her lap, pushing herself back into the chair. "Is there an update on Mateo yet? Does he remember anything?"

Paige was trying to gauge if the sincerity in Molly's voice was an act. "I just came back in, and Martha over there looked like she would rather wrestle a bear, so I decided to see if you knew anything first."

Molly glanced at the nurses station and back at Paige. "Good call." The corner of her mouth inched up.

"What I can't figure out is how he got the cut on his head if he was wearing his helmet," Paige mused.

Molly opened her mouth to answer, but was interrupted. "That is something I would also like to know."

Scott stood there with his biceps bulging under his fire company t-shirt and arms folded across a chiseled chest. His jaw was set as he glared at Molly. Paige tore her gaze away from him as Molly jumped to her feet.

Paige pushed off her knees as she stood, feeling the exhaustion from the day, then she took a small step away to give Molly some space. She hoped that Molly would tell them something to figure out what happened in that house.

Chapter 5

S COTT FELT PAIGE TAKE a step away from Molly and closer to him. He wasn't sure if the move was a sign of trust or if she just wanted a better view of Molly's face as she answered their questions. Scott gave himself a mental shake and focused solely on Molly.

"Cruz and I were headed towards the second floor to help Tucker and Jones search. When I got halfway up the stairs, I noticed that Mateo wasn't behind me anymore. I retraced my steps and found him on the floor. That's when I radioed in and you know the rest." Molly's words came out in a rush, but her tone rang with truth.

Scott gave Paige a glance to read her reaction. She was stone solid, giving nothing away.

"Did Cruz have his helmet on when you found him?" Paige asked and placed her hands on her hips.

"No. It was beside him." Molly shifted. "I put it back on him before I hooked him into my harness. Why?"

Instead of answering her question, Paige asked another. "You cleaned the wound. Was there anything strange in it besides soot?"

"I...I don't recall." Molly stumbled over her words. "What's going on?"

Scott spoke up. "We just want to make sure what happened was just an accident."

"I didn't see anyone else in the house that wasn't a firefighter, and Tucker had called an all clear for the first floor." Molly flopped back down in the plastic seat. "I pray that Mateo is okay. He seemed pretty upset when he woke up before we arrived."

This piqued Scott's interest and explained a bit better the accusatory questions from Paige. "What did he say?"

"He was screaming, 'No', and then, 'Don't touch her' in Spanish." Paige spoke before Molly could answer.

"That's what he said?" Molly shook her head. "My Spanish isn't great."

Scott stared at this mysterious woman who found her way into the inner circle of trust in his family. She didn't miss much.

"We can cycle back to your bilingual skills later," Scott started.

"Seven."

"Excuse me?" he asked.

"I speak seven languages fluently unless you count binary as a language, then eight." Paige didn't even look at him, but stared down at Molly.

It was becoming clearer why Rachel and his dad would allow her to be close. She certainly was not your average computer geek paramedic. In short, she was impressive and his respect for her grew more.

Scott turned his focus back to Molly. "Molly, you're sure you didn't see anyone? What about an object beside or near Mateo when you found him?"

"I'm sure I didn't see anyone but other firefighters. I briefly looked for an object when I found him, but didn't see anything unusual." She ran her fingers through her hair. "That's why I radioed in the mechanism of injury unknown. I was more worried about getting him out of the burning building first before investigating the surrounding area. That will have to be the job of the police if you think that's necessary."

He wasn't going to get more out of Molly, and other firefighters were starting to arrive. That was the beautiful thing about being a part of the fire company, everyone was family and when one was injured, they all felt it.

Scott took a step toward the corner of the waiting area and motioned for Paige to follow him. When they got far enough away, Scott leaned close to keep their conversation confidential. "What is your take on Molly and her account of what happened?"

"From her body language and voice inflections, she's telling the truth. Which means that unless some random person ran into a burning house, another firefighter hit Mateo over the head," she stated as if an expert on interrogation.

"I would tend to believe the latter." Tucker was in a clean company polo and cargo pants, but soot was smudged across his cheek.

Paige swung around to face him. Next to him, she seemed small in height and breadth, but she held her ground, rising to her full height.

"What do you know, Tucker?" Paige demanded.

Scott had to work hard not to laugh at her take-charge personality. It wasn't humorous, but in a crazy way, her passion about the people around her gave him joy. That was one thing he hadn't been able to find since that night long ago.

She looked over her shoulder at him. "This isn't funny."

Scott wiped any smile he had from his face. "You're right. Tucker?"

"Once I heard the call across the radio, I made sure that all the teams were where they were supposed to be. I came downstairs as Molly was dragging Mateo out the door. Before I went back up the steps to help, I checked out the area where she dragged him from." Tucker paused as if he wanted to add suspense.

"And?" Paige drew out the word.

"Given that the rest of the house was well put together, it was strange that I found a table lamp on the floor over by the opposite wall from the hallway table. It's possible that one of the crew knocked it over, but I wanted to secure it just in case."

Tucker blew out a breath. Scott could tell that there was more and he probably was not going to like it.

"I took the lamp outside and decided I would take care of it once we had the fire under control. When I came back out to get it, it had disappeared. I checked the whole property as much as I could. Nothing."

Clearly, whoever did this hoped the lamp and the evidence on it would have burned in the fire, or at least, had the water destroy anything they left behind. They were smart, but the why was still what he didn't understand.

Scott shifted tactics. "Tell me about Mateo. Does he have any enemies in the company?"

"None that I can tell." Tucker sighed. "He just graduated from high school last year. I know that Marcus gave him a job as a mover for his moving company at the start of the summer. He uses most of his income to help pay for his mother's medical expenses; she has been receiving cancer treatments and her insurance covers very little of it. From what I can tell, he seems like a good kid just trying to help his mom and his community."

Tucker's description of the man left them with more questions than answers. Who would want to harm Mateo? Especially a fellow firefighter? A brother, or sister, in arms?

The doors to outside swished open as a small woman who looked frail yet stalwart all at the same time held onto Tylan's arm as they entered. This must be Mateo's mother.

In a blink of an eye, Paige was by her side. She talked to her in Spanish with hushed tones. Scott only caught words or phrases as she spoke. He would need to work on his Spanish. Language acquisition was something his dad tried unsuccessfully to train him in. Sure, he knew key words and phrases in many different languages, but watching Paige converse so fluidly in another language made him want to do better.

"Gracias, Paige." The woman turned to him. "You must be the new fire chief. Your mother has told me many good things about you."

She paused for a moment and Scott absorbed the fact she knew who his mother was. New Freedom was bigger than when he left, but it was still a smaller town. It shouldn't surprise him that she would know her.

She placed her free hand on his arm and tugged him closer. "This is not your fault. I know you will find out what happened to my boy."

Her intense stare made Scott want to pull away, but he gave her a sharp nod.

"I will Mrs...." Scott realized then that he didn't even know the woman's name.

"Sofia De Maria Cruz." She patted his arm again. "You may call me Sofia. Your mother was the first person in town to make us feel welcome. She is a good woman." Sofia's eyes began to shine. "I am sorry for what happened to her. I will be praying for your whole family."

Mention of his mother's condition made his stomach tighten. "Thank you," was all he could squeeze out of his throat.

Scott felt a determination settle in his soul. He would find out what happened to all three of them. Looking straight at Tylan, a silent agreement passed between the two of them. Scott knew that Tylan would help him figure out everything.

Paige shifted and again Scott was taken back by how his body responded to her presence. When she drew near to him, he had to force himself to focus harder because his mind wanted to focus on the sweet smattering of freckles across her high cheekbones, which drew attention to her emerald eyes.

He hadn't dated anyone since that night. *Women were a distraction.* He needed to keep his head in the game. This town trusted him and he wasn't about to let himself be distracted by anything, even if it was a beautiful woman.

Paige stood next to Scott as Tylan helped Sofia over to the nurses station to get an update on Mateo. If he only took a half-step to his left, their arms would be touching. The thought made him take a step away and turn to face her again. Space was good.

"Don't even think about cutting me out," she said in a terse whisper.

"Don't take this the wrong way, but why? I don't even know you besides what Tucker here has told me."

She held her chin high as if she defied any sting his words held over her. She cut her gaze to Tucker, who raised his eyebrows and showed his hands in a sign of surrender. Her hands dropped to her hips and she lowered her chin.

"Look, we may not know each other, but your parents are the closest thing to a family that I have." Her words stirred a want for him to protect her, although she probably didn't need or want his protection. "And, try as I may to stay isolated, this fire company is fast becoming a community to me. I know it may sound crazy, but I think there is something going on here and these accidents could be connected."

He had the same thought, but wanted to hear her theory. More firefighters were showing up to check on one of their own.

"Let's meet tomorrow morning. In my office at 0800."

Both Tucker and Paige nodded in agreement.

Dr. Felton walked through the doors and stopped short. "Family of Mateo Cruz?"

Sofia called from close to the nurses station, "Here, but these are his brothers and sisters of the fire company."

Dr. Felton gave a knowing grin and addressed her, but was loud enough for everyone to hear. "Mateo is doing well and will be discharged soon. He has stitches where he was hit, but the CT showed only a minor concussion."

"Praise Jesus for hearing our prayers," Sofia squeaked behind a suppressed sob.

"If you follow me back, ma'am, the nurse will be in soon with discharge papers and instructions." Dr. Felton placed a hand on her back and guided her towards the doors.

Sofia turned to everyone in the waiting room before entering the hall. "Thank you all for coming."

Scott stepped forward. "If you or Mateo need anything, especially in the next few days, please call me."

He dug into his wallet and pulled out one of his new business cards his mother had made for him when he told her that he accepted the job. It was like she knew that he would need them before he even officially started.

"I will." She took the card and placed it in her pocket.

"Bryson and Bryant," Scott barked, then softened his tone. "Will you make sure the Cruzs get home safely?"

Kent and Molly stepped forward and waited by the doors to the ER. Everyone else started to leave the waiting room. It was after midnight and all of the volunteers had other jobs that they had to do in the morning.

It was both a drawback and strength of a volunteer company like the one they had in New Freedom. It made scheduling shifts and finding coverage to be a challenge, but every single one of the volunteers were there because they were dedicated to their community.

Scott was almost to his fire chief truck when he heard footsteps behind him. Spinning around on full alert, Scott stopped before striking when he saw it was Rachel.

Rachel smirked. "I see you still have your lightning quick reflexes."

Scott deflated. "What are you still doing here?"

"I know a few people who pulled a few strings and let me stay with Mom." She flipped her hand as if it was no big deal.

Scott narrowed his eyes at his sister.

"Okay, okay. I may have told them that I needed to stay close to keep her safe since she may or may not have been the target. It helped that Tylan or Ronnie had been outside our room all evening."

Scott wasn't sure he wanted the answer, but he needed to know. "How are they?"

"Mom is still unconscious. Dad is in a medically-induced coma after surgery. They were able to stop all the internal bleeding, but his heart stopped one more time on the table. It will be touch and go for a few days. They were able to put their rooms next to each other."

"I was going to head to the cabin to get some sleep." Scott felt the exhaustion from the day deep in his bones. "You should join me. I'm sure that they will be fine overnight. I'll bring you back first thing in the morning."

Indecision warred in her eyes as she looked between the hospital and him. When she stopped her roaming gaze on the bed of the truck, she took a step towards it.

She peered over the edge. "Why do you have two sets of turnout gear in your truck?"

"One is mine and the other is Mateo's."

She spun to face him. "Are you saying that Mateo was injured under suspicious circumstances?"

Scott glanced around the dark parking lot. "Let's talk more about this at the cabin."

"Fine." Rachel opened the passenger door, climbed in, and slammed it shut.

They rode the entire trip in silence. It was anything but a comfortable silence that siblings could share. He wasn't sure what he said to make her so mad. He was hoping that he could chalk it up to her exhaustion. Scott ran through everything that happened since this morning.

Rachel interrupted his thoughts. "You know, it has been hard growing up in the shadow of your absence. You were the brave one. The soldier who was a decorated hero. You fly into wildfires, which is ranked in the top five most dangerous jobs, by the way."

She rested her head on the seat and stared at the truck roof. "Dad only saw me as a fragile thing needing protection."

Scott mentally winced because he had thought the same thing only today. He stopped the truck by the cabin and faced her.

"I don't think Dad saw you as fragile, but he knew the evil in the world and how insanely smart you are. He didn't want to see you taken and forced to do things that no one should do."

His words made him think of Heather. What things was she forced to do? He said a quick prayer for her as he did most days.

Rachel touched his arm. "You know no one thinks it is your fault, right?"

Scott grunted. "Let's get inside."

He followed Rachel up the steps. The cabin looked older, but well maintained. It gave the impression that it was bare necessities inside, but also used frequently. The latter was true. Inside of the cabin, though, was much more than bare necessities.

Rachel unlocked the door and he stepped into the familiar space. The piney scent from his mother's favorite cleaner enveloped him as he wandered into the open living, dining, and kitchen area.

The couch and recliner were new but the pillows Rachel and he had made still adorned the couch. The kitchen had the same formica countertop, but the cabinets were repainted and a backsplash was installed.

"I like what Mom did with the place. It looks good."

Rachel snorted. "I have been living here, thank you."

Scott spun around to face her. "Oh, Mom said that I could stay here until I found my own place."

Rachel stared at him with annoyance. "There is more than one bedroom, but I have the master room with the en suite bathroom."

Scott shrugged. "As long as you are good with this."

"It's fine." Rachel crossed her arms. "Now, tell me why you have Mateo's turn out gear."

He was hoping she would have forgotten about that, but he should have known better than to think that his genius sister would forget anything.

Scott briefly explained to her what he knew about what happened that night during the fire.

"Well, this confirms it then."

Rachel's statement threw him off. "Confirms what, exactly?"

"Mateo and I are...friends and he seemed off the past few days." She let her arms fall to her sides. "I tried to get him to tell me what was going on. He said as soon as he figured it out he would tell the right people, but begged me to stay out of it."

Respect for Mateo grew. "Do you have any idea what he is talking about?"

"No. He is one of the good guys, Griz. I wish he would have trusted me."

"I don't think it has anything to do with trusting you. I think he was trying to be careful. Clearly, whatever it is was important enough to make an attempt on his life."

Scott put the gear on the dining room table. "I brought this home so that I could go over it to make sure that the equipment wasn't malfunctioning. I need to rule out all possibilities before I go around investigating the men in the company."

Scott rubbed his hand down his face. Exhaustion was tugging at him as the adrenaline was leaving his system.

Rachel put her hand on his forearm. "Why don't we both get a few hours of sleep and then look over the equipment together before you take me back to the hospital?"

Scott kissed her forehead. "You're right, baby sis."

"Please don't call me that." Rachel rolled her eyes and headed for her room.

Scott looked at the equipment one more time before heading to his own room with his overnight bag. He would get his duffel from his own truck tomorrow when he returned to the station with the chief's truck.

As he laid in the soft queen bed, he thought about the day.

His parents were run off the road. Why?

Mateo was injured in the fire. Was it an accident or did he know something he wasn't supposed to?

He rolled these questions around in his mind as he drifted into sleep. Tomorrow would hopefully bring some answers.

Chapter 6

"*O*NLY ONE MORE MONTH, Doc." *Hank circled her waist and brought her close to him. She rested her head against his chest, completely content despite the destruction, searing heat, and utter despair surrounding them.*

He cleared his throat, breaking her bubble of happiness. She spun to face him. "You have a mission, don't you?"

He said nothing. She had been the medic embedded with his unit for the whole deployment, which she had thanked God for every day. So why didn't she know about this mission?

"MacFarland!"

Before she could turn away, he whispered, "One last mission. Pray for us."

She walked toward Command. When she looked back, he was gone and a pile of ashes blew into her face. Blinking her eyes, she saw their helicopter explode and crash to the ground.

Paige sat up in her bed and put her hands to her eyes, willing the tears to stay where they were. She was done crying. Yesterday's events had her feeling like she did back then. Worried about those she cared about. Confused about what exactly was going on.

And alone.

For two years she was fine on her own, not getting attached to people. If you let no one in, then you wouldn't have the gut-wrenching nightmares of losing them. Here she was, though, eight months in New Freedom and already attached to the Craftons and the fire department.

She threw back the cover and checked the clock. 0600.

She hadn't realized how tired she was. Her shift was over in an hour. Making quick work of her bunk and getting ready, Paige made her way to the kitchen. She couldn't cook many things, but coffee, bacon, and eggs she had mastered.

The smells wafted through the station, drawing out the other men and women on her shift. The crew took their food and sat at the table or stood around the kitchen island.

Bryson, who clearly needed more coffee, rubbed his eyes. "Did anyone get an update on Mateo?"

Marcus set his fork down and took a swig of his brew. "He texted this morning. Said his mother is driving him crazy already and he hopes to be cleared by the docs soon so he can work his next shift on Friday."

Concussions were no joke, even minor ones. Paige highly doubted that he would be back in three days. At least, not back in full capacity.

She checked her watch—only fifteen minutes left of her shift. She jumped up and headed towards the bay. The last thing she did on every shift was double-check her rig and restock anything that it needed as well as return her jump bag fully stocked to the locker. Two things she didn't do last night.

"Marcus, it's you and Bryson for clean-up duty." She called over her shoulder as she disappeared out the door. The men's disappointing grunts made her smile.

Lost in her thoughts and mental checklist, Paige slammed into a wall at the end of the hall. Looking up, she was caught off guard by the bluest eyes she'd ever seen. The bright blue fire chief polo he wore pushed the gray to the side and pulled the blue hues forward. They were bright, tempting, and held a bit of mischief.

"I...I'm sorry," she stammered.

Her stutter earned her a lopsided grin. "No worries."

As if reading the questions in her eyes, he lifted the duffel higher on his shoulder. "I came in early to look over Mateo's gear and meet more of the crew at shift change."

Noticing that they were still standing close to each other, Paige took a step away. "Well, don't let me stand in your way."

"Would you like to look over the gear with me?"

"Afraid you might miss something?" Paige couldn't stop the quip. She was talking to a superior, not a friend. She opened her mouth to apologize when Scott started to laugh. His laugh was full and deep. She wanted to feel slighted that he was laughing at her, but it washed over her, peeling back some of the stress.

"I'm sorry," he finally said as his laughter subsided.

"This is the second time you have found my seriousness funny." She put her hands on her hips.

His eyes opened in shock briefly before he gained control. "I'm not laughing at you. I just find your take charge, knock the doors down, all in, caring spirit refreshing." His face turned somber. "I've lived for too long without joy in my life. Still not certain that I deserve it, but I'm trying."

Paige felt a bond strengthen between them. Whatever he went through, he knew about pain and loss.

"Well, in that case, I will continue to be, as my CO once said, 'A stubborn sarcastic Corpsman'. And to actually answer your question, I've got to check my jump bag back into the locker, then I'll come give a second opinion on the gear."

As she gathered everything and signed her bag back into the locker, she let her mind wander over the events of yesterday. First, Charles and Paola were forced off the road. There was clearly a set of tire tracks going away from the scene of the accident. And Charles' cryptic message, *'The sparrow has flown, help Rachel find her'.*

"Who is the sparrow?" she whispered to herself.

She would make a mental note to ask Rachel once she was done talking with Scott and Tucker. Since her shift was officially over and all of her gear was returned, Paige opted to change into her favorite outfit of jeans and a t-shirt complete with sarcastic or pun-filled saying. Feeling more like herself, she made her way to Scott's office.

She knocked on the door.

"Come in." The rich deep tone of his voice drew in her heart.

She needed to get herself together. Every person she let in died and left her alone. Securing the walls around her heart, she entered the small office.

Amusement danced in Scott's eyes as he read her t-shirt that said, 'There are 10 kinds of people: those that understand binary and those that don't'. Although, this time he controlled himself and did not laugh. She was glad because his laughter would have put another crack in the wall around her heart.

"Did you find anything with his gear?" she asked.

The amusement was replaced by a strict focus she was starting to associate with him as the fire chief. "I want you to take a look at his SCBA mask."

Paige picked the mask and regulator off the desk. She had never had to wear one in the field, but was fitted for one during her training. Taking in every detail, she roamed her fingers over the seals and facepiece lens. Along the left side was a small crack.

"There is a crack here. Was that caused by the impact of whatever hit him?"

Scott shrugged. "I'm not a forensic expert, but Tylan might know someone we could trust."

"Why don't we just turn this over to the police?"

Scott walked past her and closed the door. "Until I know what happened, I don't want to cause alarm. Besides, the state lab, as well as the police, are backed up. Without proof of a crime, they won't do anything."

The bitter edge to his voice made her curious. Did the by-the-book fire chief not trust the police?

"If the crack was there before the blow to the head, Mateo could have been weakened already and not been able to defend himself fully." Paige put her thoughts out there, but saying it made this situation even more dark.

"That is my concern as well."

A foreboding was churning in her as her mind raced with possible scenarios. What could he have done or seen that would make him a target?

A knock at the door cut off her thoughts. "Come in," Scott called.

The greeting this time stirred in her a different kind of anticipation. One that made her adrenaline start to pump. Who could she trust? Charles told her to trust Scott. She looked at the man before turning towards the door. He had done nothing but show he could be trusted. She would do well to keep her heart guarded, but she would enlist his help to find the sparrow too.

Tucker stepped through the door and she felt herself relax a bit. "I see you started the party without me." Tucker took the seat next to her.

Tucker and Scott were both about the same height, a foot taller than her five-four frame. They both had broad shoulders, trim waists, and bulging muscles a side effect of the continuous training, hauling heavy equipment and competitive workouts among the firefighters.

Although that was where their similarities ended. Where Scott had blue eyes, tanned skin, and sandy-blond hair, Tucker was the epitome of tall, dark, and handsome. His black hair was cropped short, his eyes were the color of walnut wood, and his dark bronze skin made many women swoon. His attractiveness, though, never threatened to crack her self-protective walls like Scott did.

"Tucker, thanks for coming."

Scott pulled his chair towards the small couch that sat against the wall next to the door where Paige and Tucker were seated. Paige sat closer to the corner of the wall. *Always pick the seat where you can watch the door.* Hank's words filtered through her head. He was in her dreams and now in her waking moments. For the first time though, a reminder of him didn't send her spiraling.

She was proud of herself and then realized that she had no one to share this momentous occasion with because she never told anyone about Hank or her Móraí or her parents. In fact, the only person she ever talked to any length about what happened was the appointed counselor they made her see afterwards. It was just a box to check to get back into the field. The problem was she didn't want to be a part of a group anymore. What was the point when everyone died and left her?

She snapped herself back to reality as Scott said, "I think we can all agree that something is going on in the fire company."

"It's clear to me that Mateo didn't hit himself over the head with the lamp, but I just can't figure out why." Tucker turned toward her on the couch. "You haven't heard anything or other people talking have you?"

"Honestly, I like to keep to myself. I'm not great with idle chit-chat or drama." Paige wanted to contribute so she continued, "but I can go to Mateo's house when I get off. I can ask him what he remembers."

A knock at the door interrupted her next question about an update on Scott's parents.

Scott stood and walked toward the door. Opening it, Paige couldn't believe what she saw. David Weller, Mayor of New Freedom, standing there in his signature three piece suit, blue tie, and American flag pin. He was a politician through and through.

What in the world could he want? Paige had a general distrust of all politicians after living in DC for a year, no matter that he was a mayor of a small town. Politicians, in her opinion, were all the same.

"Mayor, can I help you?"

"I came to speak with you." David's smooth voice had won the trust of many voters, but it made her want to cringe.

"Of course." Scott stepped back to let him in. "Do you mind the Assistant Chief and Lead Paramedic being present for our conversation?"

Lead Paramedic, she liked the sound of that. Scott clearly knew how the political game worked. This was his office, but he was giving Weller the courtesy of making a choice. Smooth.

"They can stay." His words sounded like he was talking about a pet, which grated on Paige's nerves. She balled her fists and reminded herself to bite her tongue.

Scott offered the mayor his chair, but the man declined. Paige was amused. The man was only five eleven at best. Scott's six-four frame probably made him feel small. She also noticed that Scott never took his seat either. He just went up a few spots in her book.

"What can I help you with?"

"I just wanted to come by and congratulate you on a job well done yesterday. I was told that one man got injured, but that your team worked well together and were able to save a portion of the home. How is the injured firefighter?"

Scott shifted his weight and relaxed his shoulders. "He was sent home last night. He has a minor concussion and some stitches, but he will be back on his feet soon."

"Good. I know it's your first day, but I would like to meet with you to discuss the state of the department soon. I promised the people of New Freedom that I would support our fire department. So take a week, and bring me a report about what you see, and where you would like to improve."

Scott's back stiffened. "Of course, sir. I will call your secretary next week and set up an appointment."

"Good, good. I must go. See you next week with your report."

Without waiting for anyone to give him a salutation, he left.

Paige just shook her head.

"Care to share your thoughts?" Scott pinned her with his gaze.

"I don't like politicians. Spent only a year in DC and I've had my fill."

"I've been told that he is a big supporter of the fire department," Scott countered.

Tucker grunted. "It's all about control."

Scott tilted his head and waited for Tucker to continue.

"He could have just as easily called you or sent you an email requesting that report and meeting, but he showed up here." Tucker conceded

"It's true. He didn't even sit when you offered your chair," Paige added.

Tucker seemed to fidget as if the conversation was becoming uncomfortable.

"I don't want any secrets between me and my assistant chief." Scott held his stare. "What you say inside these walls stays here."

"I can leave if..." Paige began to stand, but Tucker put a hand on her arm to stop her.

"I trust you."

Those three words were like honey and dynamite. Soothing, but deadly to her isolated existence. Paige sat back down and waited to hear what Tucker was thinking.

"I don't want to speak ill of the dead, but about a month before Chief Fox died, the mayor would come in two or three times a week. At first I didn't think anything of it, but..." Tucker flexed his fists. "Two days before the accident, Weller was in this office yelling at Fox. I couldn't hear what they were arguing about, but Fox wasn't himself the rest of his shift."

"Are you saying that Mayor Weller is dirty?" Scott's voice held no accusation.

"Not necessarily, but the man likes to get his own way. Before you accept any campaign promises from him, know that it will come with strings attached."

Scott nodded. "Understood."

The two started going over what the company did well and where they saw needs for improvements. Paige felt her phone vibrate in her pocket, indicating she had a text message.

She unlocked the phone to see who was contacting her. Rollands.

Meet me at the fountain. 1600.

No explanation on why he hadn't checked in yesterday. Not like she was responsible for his well-being, but the daily check-in had become a reassurance. Now that she knew he sent her to Crafton to be protected, his absence yesterday gave her pause for concern.

I'll be there, she texted back.

Paige stood. "You both don't need me to review the company, and I need to get back to my day job."

Scott looked like he wanted to ask her what that job was, but he decided against it. Smart man because she wouldn't be able to tell him even if she wanted to.

Paige left the station and decided to go home instead of Mateo's. If she was going to meet with Rollands, she should make some progress on the code. She was close to finishing it. When it was time, she would test it on a secure network at a government facility, but she didn't want to make that trip until she knew she was ready.

Driving out toward her camper on the Craftons' land, she passed by the place where the car accident occurred. She needed to tell Scott about his father's cryptic message. Charles said she could trust him and she was starting to believe that.

Glancing in the rearview mirror, she noticed a black SUV following her. She got off one exit before her own and rolled through the stop sign at the end of the ramp. A few seconds later the black SUV appeared in her mirror again. Great.

It was looking like she would need to use those defensive driving skills that Hank insisted she learn. She remembered rolling her eyes at him and asking when she would ever need defensive driving skills. The memory made her smile as she accelerated.

"You want to follow me? You'll have to keep up."

The black SUV sped up to keep pace. Right before she reached the top of the mountain there was an old logging road. She had requested a map of the area when she moved in, and memorized all of the roads no matter how small. It would test her driving skills and her car's four wheel drive, but chances were she could lose the tail before then. The SUV was almost on her bumper. Their engine was bigger than the one in her little hatchback.

Seeing the road that would connect her to the logging road approaching quickly, she punched the accelerator one last time, pulled the parking brake, and made the turn. The SUV flew past the road, but the screeching of brakes indicated that they were going to be coming back. She needed to put as much distance between them and her as possible.

Instead of trying to make it the whole way to the logging road, she saw a grove of young trees off the side of the road covered in mile-a-minute weed. That would provide enough cover for her car. She eased her way into the grove and cut her engine.

She took a few deep breaths to calm her racing heart and reclined her seat. Why were those guys following her? Did it have to do with Rollands' message? The Craftons? She squeezed her eyes shut and listened for the drone of a passing car. She was alone and for the first time, she wished she wasn't.

Chapter 7

S COTT HAD SPENT THE last hour pouring over the rosters and equipment inventory files that had not been updated for some time. He would have his work cut out for him in bringing everything current by next Wednesday.

It was clear, though, based on what he witnessed last night, that the volunteers were well trained. Although, he believed that to be the work of Tucker rather than the former chief.

Tucker would be a great ally in his transition here, as would Paige. An image of her standing in his door filtered through his head. He wasn't sure if she knew how beautiful she was. She seemed to have her heart locked down tighter than Fort Knox, but he could tell that she cared deeply about people.

Scott shook the image from his head; women were a distraction and right now he had plenty on his plate. Even thinking about a woman was not within his mental capacity, despite the fact that she was the first to even push past his mental barrier in the past twelve years.

During his service, his fellow airmen called him Monk because he never drank when they went out, and even if a woman flirted with him, he always turned her down. It wasn't that he didn't like women or didn't notice them, but the last woman he was with made him lose focus. At that moment, someone else under his care disappeared.

Scott's phone started to talk to him. "Pick up the phone, Griz, it's your sister."

What in the world? Scott swiped to receive the call. "Hello?"

"Do you like the ringtone I made for you?" Rachel sounded upbeat.

"I thought my phone was being possessed, but I'll keep it. What's up, kid?"

"You really need to give me a new nickname." She huffed.

"Rachel." Annoyance crept into his voice.

"Fine. I thought you should know that Mom is waking up."

Scott didn't even let her finish. "I'll be right there."

Hanging up, he shoved the phone in his pocket and made his way to his personal truck. He texted Tucker to let him know that he was on his way to the hospital. Tucker technically had the day off, but he felt like he should let someone know.

Scott parked in the guest lot at the hospital a few moments later and jogged into the building. He slowed to a walk once inside. No need to draw any unwanted attention to himself. He pushed the button for the elevator, but decided it was moving too slowly and took the stairs to the fourth floor.

Because it was the ICU, there was a station in front of a set of double doors. Each patient was only allowed two visitors, and you needed to register at the desk. As he opened his mouth to give his name, the double doors swooshed open.

"Why'd you hang up on me?" Rachel's accusatory tone cut through the silence. "If you would have listened to me, you would know that she is out for a CT scan and won't be back for a while."

"I wanted to be here for her."

Rachel rolled her eyes. "You are so much like Dad."

Scott wasn't sure if he wanted to be like his father or not. Sure, he had forgiven him for not being there when Scott needed him most, but he didn't want that to be his legacy.

"They said that they are hoping to bring him out of the medically-induced coma either later today or tomorrow." Rachel stepped in front of him as he put his visitor badge on. "You should go see him. He can hear things even through the coma."

This wasn't what he came here to do, but maybe this was God's way of forcing him to deal with the past.

The rooms for the ICU were set up in a U shape around a massive nurses station and medical supply locker which was only accessible by keycode and card swipe. Scott made his way to the far curve where his father and mother had rooms next to each other. The curtain was drawn to his father's room and Scott took in a deep breath filling his lungs with the potent smell of sanitary cleaner.

Pulling back the curtain Scott could see his dad laying in a large bed with tubes and wires connected at various places. The once giant in his life looked so frail. His chest squeezed as he took it all in.

Rachel appeared at his side, "You know you inspired him."

Scott whipped his head toward her, "What? The great and mighty Charles Crafton was inspired by the boy who got someone killed?"

Rachel narrowed her eyes. "You really believe that, don't you?"

"Heather disappeared while I was supposed to be watching her, and after seeing the evils of this world, it would be more merciful for her to have died." Scott felt the weight of the past pull down his shoulders and press in his lungs.

"If she was sold for slave labor or, even worse, sex trafficked, her life would have been torture. I've seen the aftermath. I've witnessed truckloads of people diseased, broken, dying. They are moved from place to place being held by fear or manipulation. I pray she didn't have to go through that."

Rachel's eyes searched his face. "I promised Dad I would let him tell you. Stubborn man, wasted years holding this secret."

"What are you talking about, Rach?"

"Rach is a much better nickname." She quirked a smile.

"Focus," he groused.

"Right, we can't talk about it in an unsecured location. If we go home, I can show you the security footage I gave to the police and we could maybe get a glimpse of who did this to Mom and Dad."

It looked like he would have to wait until his dad woke up before he got his answers.

He turned towards his father's bed. Laying a hand on his foot, he whispered, "I'll watch over them, but you've got to pull through this. Don't die on us."

He stepped away and nodded at Rachel. "Let's go home."

"I want to leave a note for Mom at the nurses station to let her know we'll come back after lunch." Rachel spun and left the room.

"I'm going to call Tylan to keep watch." Scott pulled out his phone, trailing after Rachel.

Scott and Rachel pulled into the long lane of the cabin after the twenty minute drive from the hospital. Strange how he only slept here one night, but it was already starting to feel like home.

Rachel brought two computers out to the dining table and sat next to Scott. "This is Dad's computer. We have our own VPN."

"Where are we pinging from today?"

"It's best if you don't know, that way you cannot be held accountable for knowledge you do not have."

"I don't like the sound of that," Scott grunted. What was his dad into?

"With our line of work, being a ghost online is a must. Now let me log you in."

Only two types of people needed to be ghosts online, the good guys who were living amongst, fighting against, or trying to take down the evil of this world, and those who are doing that evil. Given his father's past, Scott was fairly confident that his father fell into the former category. What he couldn't figure out is why his dad let Rachel into his kind of work. Growing up, she was always the protected and Scott the protector.

The number of questions he had for his dad was growing by the minute. He said a quick prayer that he was able to be taken out of his coma soon.

Rachel scanned her finger and then typed in a password. The double layer of security was smart. It would deter most criminals and seriously slow down the most determined.

"So, are you going to tell me now what you and Dad do for your line of work?" Scott knew that bringing the question back up was a long shot, but he had to try.

"Nope. Dad said he wanted to be the one to tell you. I promised him I would respect his wishes."

Her fingers paused over her own keyboard and looked up at him. "But if he doesn't pull through, I will tell you. I promise."

She dropped her eyes back to her screen. His heart squeezed at the possibility. Charles Crafton was a fighter, but the body could only take so much before it quit. Even though he hadn't talked with his dad in twelve years, Scott was having a hard time imagining a world without his dad in it.

Bringing himself out of that spiraling train of thought, Scott pulled up the feed from their parents' house. He watched a hooded figure pick the lock on the front door and let themselves in. About 20 minutes later, they left the same way with their head down and hood pulled low.

"I wish Dad had installed cameras inside the house."

Rachel snorted. "You know Dad. The man likes to be safe, but he values his privacy more. And with the right hacker, even the best defense can be penetrated. That's why he wants Paige."

"Why would Dad want Paige?"

Rachel looked anywhere but at him. "Let's just say that Paige's computer skills are the best of the best. She is even better than me, which is hard for me to admit."

On the large TV screen, Rachel had put the cameras from the cabin property on display. There was movement in the north woods. Someone was trying to sneak onto their property.

"Rachel, I need you to head to the bunker."

Her head snapped toward the TV. "It would be better if we both go."

"No." Scott used his best CO voice. "I promised Dad I would keep you safe. Now go."

He knew he was a bit harsh with Rachel, but he could apologize when he secured the property. Without giving her another opportunity to argue with him, Scott grabbed his sidearm from his duffel and headed for the supply shed to get the UTV, banking on his dad keeping it in good condition all these years. He would take it up the back path, park about halfway, and then go the rest of the way on foot.

His phone dinged, indicating that he received a message. Pulling it out, Rachel had sent him a text.

Rachel: *I'm not a little girl anymore.*

Eyes: 3068:g9n0:5006:945::650j

He clicked on the IP and the camera feeds for that section of the property filled the screen. Whoever this was had a baseball cap pulled down over their eyes and was moving with stealth. Bonus for him, they clearly had no knowledge of the cameras.

When he left, he had just helped his dad install three cameras. His father was either becoming more paranoid or he was doing something that warranted the heightened security. Scott's guess was the latter.

Scott arrived at the shed and was faced with a brand new keypad entry. He texted Rachel.

Scott: *Key code?*

Rachel: *You should have taken me with you.*

Rachel: *I'm not a child. I'll be 23 on my next birthday.*

Scott hoped that he was reading her text correctly, and punched in her birthday plus her age. When the door clicked open, he breathed a sigh of relief. He would have to thank her later.

Flipping the switch to illuminate the shed, Scott let out a low whistle. This UTV was not the same one he had saved his money for and bought off of old Mr. Miller. The UTV in front of him was state of the art with all kinds of additional gadgets, including cell phone holder and Bluetooth.

Scott found the keys on the wall and started off towards the north woods, praying that whomever he met up there would not get past him to Rachel.

He stopped part way up the mountain and hid the UTV off the road. Checking the camera feed one more time, he knew that the intruder was about one klick directly north of his location. They were following beside the dirt path, only using the woods for cover.

These woods were like a second home to Scott. He had spent countless hours training, playing, and camping in them. Calling on all of the skills his father and the Air Force taught him, Scott made his way silently through the trees.

Once he found the perfect spot, he waited. Listened.

There. About twenty yards to his left he heard them. They were good, but he no doubt still had the element of surprise. He slipped from his spot and got into position about ten yards in front of them.

Eight yards.

Six yards.

The woman stopped about five yards out. He could tell from this distance that it was indeed a woman, but he knew many women that could be just as dangerous as any man.

Suddenly, she took off in a sprint away from him. He held back a curse and pounced from his hiding spot. She was fast, but no match for his longer legs. Leaping into the air, Scott aimed for her waist and legs, wrapping his large arms around her, bringing her to the ground swiftly.

They rolled, barely missing a large oak tree. Roots and stones greeted him as he rolled away from the intruder. Scott sprang to his feet, readying himself for the fight to come. The woman swung her leg, but Scott was faster.

With one smooth move, he grabbed her ankle and flipped her over.

In the tumble, she lost her hat and when she whipped her head up, Scott froze. He dropped her leg. "Paige? What the...? Why are you sneaking onto my parents' property?"

Relief flooded her eyes, and for a moment, she slumped against the dirt. As quickly as she relaxed, she flew to her feet.

"We have to keep moving or they will find me."

"Wait. They who?"

"I don't know. I don't even know why they are chasing me, but thankfully they are not very gifted at high speed driving."

Scott had so many questions, but he knew that they could be answered later.

"I have my UTV down the path. Follow me."

They moved together through the trees and underbrush, trying to be quick while not making too much noise. An art that she was actually skilled at. Every layer he saw of her intrigued him more.

His heart wanted to peel back every barrier and get to know the mystery woman that his father sought for whatever he did and Rachel had bonded with, but his head slammed the gates shut on his wandering heart. *You have no time for distractions.*

Once they were on the UTV headed back to the cabin, Scott finally spoke.

"Okay, start at the beginning. What happened out there?"

Paige recounted the black SUV she spotted following her on the highway and how she lost them on top of the mountain.

"So you have no clue who they are or why they might be following you?"

For a moment, Paige said nothing, her expression betraying an inner struggle. She had her secrets. Didn't everyone?

"I can only think of two things. Either my line of work, which no, I cannot tell you about, or something your dad said to me."

What could have his dad told her that could have led to this? And why hadn't she told him this earlier?

"I didn't tell you about your dad's message before because at first I didn't trust you. No offense, but I didn't know you."

She tilted her head and looked at him. He stole a glance at her before returning his gaze to the dirt path. The woods were familiar, but dirt paths could change with a passing storm. He needed to get them safely back to the bunker.

"I trust you now," she said in a voice barely loud enough for him to hear over the rush of the air and motor.

"But not enough to tell me what you do for a living?" *Smooth, Scott, real smooth.*

Paige did not seem fazed by his comment. "I can tell you are a good man, but that says nothing about your government clearance level. Sorry, but I like my job."

Message received. Time to switch topics. "So what did my father tell you?"

"'*The sparrow has flown. Help Rachel find her. She can stop this. You can trust Scott.*'"

Scott's analytical brain wanted to focus on the first part about the sparrow, but his heart was stuck on the last. *You can trust Scott.*

"He was a big reason I trusted you so quickly." Paige paused. "Him and Tucker. I have come to trust both of their judgments."

A part of his wounded soul felt healing take root, but he needed to focus on the task at hand.

"Rachel is back in the bunker. I think we need to have a conversation with her when we get there. I think she knows more about my father and his work than she is willing to admit." The words left a bitter taste in his mouth, but it might be time to admit to himself that she was grown and not a little kid needing his constant protection.

The supply shed came into view. Scott pulled the UTV into its spot. He would come back later and turn it around. Right now, he needed to get Paige into the cabin and check on Rachel.

"Wow, I've never actually been inside the cabin." Paige turned in a slow circle. "From the outside, you would never know how beautiful it is inside."

Scott stopped in front of a door that looked like all of the other closet doors, but the set of stairs behind this one led to a security door. Scott scanned his hand and input his personal code. When the door released with a swoosh, he heard Paige suck in a breath. Today, she would get a crash course on a side of his family very few people knew about.

He prayed he hadn't made a mistake.

Entering another code on the reinforced steel door, Scott looked over his shoulder at Paige. "Welcome to the bunker."

They stepped through the door and Paige said in a whisper, "Whoa."

Scott felt the same way. There were definitely upgrades over the years, something he would have to admire later.

As Scott scanned the room, his gut dropped to his feet. The bunker was empty. Where was Rachel?

Chapter 8

P AIGE WASN'T ANTICIPATING THIS when she heard they were going to a bunker. In her mind, she expected metal shelves with freeze-dried foods, a crank light/radio, and a set of cots. This space was like a command center mixed with a comfortable living area. There was a large screen with multiple monitors to the side in front of a conference table. On the other wall was a small kitchen with a table for six. In between was a comfortable living space with two recliners, a couch, and TV surrounded by bookshelves.

She wanted to explore the books and discover what was behind the four doors, but one look at Scott's clenched jaw and narrow eyes kept her in her place.

"What's wrong?"

"Rachel isn't here." Scott was in soldier mode. She knew that look well.

"Could she be in one of those rooms?" She pointed to the other wall.

"One is a supply closet, the bathroom door is cracked open with no light on, and the other two are bunkrooms."

He strode quickly to the first bunkroom and shoved the door open. Finding no one, he skipped the bathroom and opened the next door. Still nothing.

Paige stepped quickly to the large monitors. "Do you know the login?"

"I doubt it's the same as it was twelve years ago." He ran his fingers through his hair.

Paige removed her pack and retrieved her tablet.

"What are you doing?" Annoyance marked his question.

"I'm trying to remember the IP address to access the cameras. Your dad gave it to me in the ambulance so that I could make sure Rachel was safe. I gave it back to her, but I think I remember it."

Scott pulled out his phone and then handed it to her. "Rachel texted it to me so that I could track the intrud...well, you across the property."

How many cameras did Charles have? Between the cameras, this bunker, and the car accident, Paige was quickly realizing that she didn't really know these people well. Could she trust them? Could she trust Scott?

"If it makes you feel better, I do not know what my father, or sister for that matter, do that warrants this kind of security. Rachel refuses to tell me and I haven't had an opportunity to ask Dad."

She wasn't sure if it was a good thing that he could anticipate her thoughts. For now, though, she needed to focus all her energy on figuring out where Rachel was.

Propping her tablet up on the conference table, she used her attached keyboard to pull up the feeds. Scott pulled one of the office chairs next to hers. Their shoulders were almost touching and the heat from his proximity made flush spread up her neck. His spicy aftershave enveloped her, causing her mind to falter briefly.

Her brain screamed to push away, but her heart begged her to stay. It felt good to be a part of a group, a family again. The dread she felt in her car less than an hour ago flashed in her mind. She wasn't sure which was worse. Being a part of a close knit group and losing everything or being completely alone and needing some backup.

"You good?" Scott's deep voice vibrated in her chest.

She shifted herself away from him slightly. Her heart longed to be a part of a community again, but that didn't mean she needed to fall for someone.

"I'm good. Give me a second to find her. It looks like your dad has most of his one hundred acres covered." She saw the cameras close to the house, but the ones she was looking at now were of the remote areas of the property, including where she hiked in from the logging road.

"I don't remember seeing cameras when I was trying to get here on foot."

Scott gave her a half grin. "My father is a master of many things. Camouflage is one of them. The cameras closer to the cabin he wanted people to see so they know someone is watching, but the ones further out are the early warning system. Unless you know where they are, you won't necessarily be able to spot them."

Paige's mind began to click things into place. "Your dad doesn't seem like the paranoid type. A patriot?"

Scott clenched his jaw. "You could call it that."

Paige stared at Scott a moment longer. The subject was clearly off limits and the conversation was over.

She clicked through the camera feeds because her screen was making it difficult to see details when all of the feeds were open. Finally, she found her.

"There. She is walking down the road. Thank God." Paige mentally chided herself. She found Rachel, not God.

"Thank God indeed."

Scott squeezed her shoulder. His touch lit her skin on fire and she stood with a rush, sending her chair rolling across the open space. "We should go get her."

She watched as hurt, concern, and then focus returned to his face.

Nice move, Doc. Hank's voice reached out to her like he was standing there with them. At that thought, a deep red flush burned her cheeks.

"Let's take my truck." Scott's words snapped her back.

She was thankful that he didn't acknowledge her reaction or ask if she was okay, because she was far from okay. The pain of Hank's loss grabbed at her composure threatening to break the dam of tears she was constantly holding at bay.

When she hadn't moved from the spot where she had stood, Scott stopped at the door and asked, "Are you coming or staying?"

His directness locked down her emotions. Paige had a feeling that the nightmares would come again tonight and then she wouldn't be able to stop the tears.

Memories of Hank had been invading her consciousness more recently. She knew it was because of the

Craftons and their openness in accepting her, but for the first time in over two years she was starting to feel whole again, as if the isolation she wore as a cloak to shield herself was no longer needed.

Paige climbed into Scott's truck. The smell of his spicy aftershave welcomed her and she involuntarily took in a deep breath. The interior was pristine.

The vehicle fit him. Strong. Dependable.

Not hauling around unnecessary baggage.

Scott blew out a breath as if he needed to confess something. "This is all my fault." He gripped the wheel. "I sent her to the bunker. Told her to stay behind."

Paige winced because she knew that Rachel was probably furious. Rachel was one of the smartest and bravest women she knew, and her biggest pet peeve was being told she couldn't do something.

"Yeah, it was a bonehead move, but I don't think I could bear the thought of losing her too."

Maybe Mr. I've-Got-It-All-Together knows a thing or two about loss. Her traitorous heart reached out to the hope that he would possibly understand the pain she carried with her.

Paige watched on the screen as Rachel stuck out her thumb. "She's trying to hitchhike."

Scott threw the truck into gear. "If something happens to her..."

Paige placed her hand on his arm, which sent a jolt of electricity through her, but she didn't move this time. "We will get there. I believe in you."

"Sometimes no matter how hard you try," he hit the dash, "evil wins in that moment. Or at least that's how it feels."

The anguish in his voice matched the anguish in her heart. A lonely tear traced down her cheek. She tried to swipe it away before he saw.

"Hey. I'm sorry." His voice softened. "Please don't cry."

Great, now he thought she was soft. She hadn't been vulnerable with anyone since the funeral. Though her therapist tried, no one was able to crack her walls and make her deal with the pain.

"I'm not crying. See?" she snapped. Then regretted it.

She blew out a breath and decided that telling him the truth, or at least part of it, might show him she wasn't fragile, but tough and someone he could depend on. "Sometimes evil does win. Sometimes God ignores your cries and allows the devil to take everything from you, until you have nothing left. So, you pick yourself back up, change careers, and move across the country."

Scott was quiet. He stole a glance at her before he began. "Your story sounds an awful lot like Job's." He paused. "Do you remember how that story ends?"

Paige scoffed. "Yeah. Job literally has nothing at the end. God could have stopped all of it, but He didn't."

"True, God could have stopped it, but Job wasn't left with nothing. Because he keeps his faith in God, God blesses him. When we are walking through the fire, God doesn't abandon us. We may not be able to see Him through the smoke, but He is still there. He loves us deeply, more than we can ever know, and He will not leave us."

"How is it loving to take everyone that I have ever loved away? The car accident that took my parents at age ten, the cancer that took my Móraí when I was overseas, unable to get home before she passed, or the RPG that blew the Blackhawk carrying the unit I had been assigned to as medic, including my fiancé? God took everyone from me." She looked out the window, refusing to see the pity on his face. "I'm all on my own now."

Another tear rolled down her opposite cheek and dripped off her chin. Telling someone about her past wasn't as terrible as she thought it would be. It actually felt good to lay it all out there. Although, now Scott would probably run in the opposite direction. She wouldn't blame him.

Scott placed his hand on her knee and squeezed. "You are not alone. God brought you here for a reason. I'm sorry for the loss you've had to endure, but you are clearly loved and trusted by my entire family."

Scott paused and removed his hand. She missed his touch.

"You've also made fast roads through my barriers, which if you ask anyone in my unit, is a miracle."

She waited to hear the story behind his walls and what exactly he meant by her making roads through them, but Rachel came into view along the road.

"I'll pull in front of her." Scott sped up.

Rachel stuck out her thumb, but recognizing the truck, her eyes narrowed and a scowl overtook her face.

"You better let me approach her first. To say she is mad is an understatement."

Paige didn't give Scott a chance to argue, but leapt out of the truck before he put it in park. Rachel's scorn turned into confusion for a fleeing moment at the sight of Paige.

"What are you doing with my brother? Wait. Are you what this is all about?" Just like that, her irritation returned. "Unbelievable. He is so much like Dad it's annoying."

Her eyes were ablaze when she faced Paige. "I am perfectly capable of taking care of myself. Mom was the only one that ever saw the fighter in me. They both think that because I'm smart, I'm helpless."

"No one thinks you're helpless, Rachel." Paige used her best bedside manner voice to calm her down. She shouted over her shoulder, "Right, Scott?"

He stood right behind her now. "You are not helpless. I..."

Paige put her hand up so that he would stop. He had created this situation and she was afraid that Rachel wasn't ready to hear his apology and reasoning.

"Rachel, your father and brother love you. You know that, right?"

"I know, but..."

Paige put her hand to stop Rachel. "Don't push them away because they underestimate you. I would give anything to have another day with any of my family."

Paige stepped forward, looping her arm through Rachel's, and spun her around to walk with her.

"I'm going to share a secret with you. Good men have this desire to protect the ones they love, no matter how capable that person is. My fiancé was the same way."

Rachel stopped and faced her. "You were engaged? What happened?"

Twice in one day she would bare at least part of her pain. Surprisingly, the pain wasn't as suffocating this time round.

"His name was Hank. We were supposed to get married in a month when he went on his last assignment." Paige blew out a breath. "I watched in horror as an RPG blew up the Blackhawk that he and his team were in. I had been embedded with them for that tour, but the mission was supposed to be information gathering to confirm a target."

"Look out!"

Scott's shout brought her out of the past in time to see a black SUV barreling towards her and Rachel. On instinct Paige grabbed Rachel, throwing her to the ground and rolling down the hill. Muddy water from the wetter than normal summer weather had gathered in the ditch, soaking through her clothes. She had no weapon on her, but that didn't mean she was defenseless.

The tall grasses obstructed her sight, but screeching tires, along with the smell of burning rubber, surrounded her, blocking out the forest that was behind them. Through the grass she could see the black vehicle roll its window down and a gun emerged. Not a gun, a taser.

Paige shoved Rachel away from her, hoping to protect her from the electricity that was to come.

"No!" Scott roared and began to shoot at the SUV. Taking fire, the driver decided to cut his losses and speed away.

In a moment, Scott was beside them, helping them out of the ditch. He scanned them both for any obvious injuries.

"I'm fine. You good, Rachel?"

"That mud is disgusting and I will probably need a long shower, but I'm good. Thanks, Paige." Rachel enveloped her in a vice-like hug. She had never received a hug from her which made this moment even more special.

Rachel pulled back and looked between the both of them. "Should we report this?"

"No."

"Probably," Scott and Paige said at the same time.

"I want to check in with my boss first. Because of the nature of my work, I want to make sure he approves reporting this." Paige hated not telling Scott more, but until she had clearance she couldn't.

"I think we should get back to the cabin, then," Scott said.

"But what about your truck?" Paige asked. She and Rachel were covered in mud and debris.

"What about it?"

"The inside looks like you just got it detailed. We are covered in mud."

Scott gave her a curious look. "Nothing much gets past you does it?"

For the second time that day, a blush crept up her neck because of him. She was torn between letting him in and guarding her heart.

Scott opened the back of the cab and reached under the seat, pulling out two old blankets. "See, no need to worry. Improvise. Adapt. Overcome," he said with a wink.

That was one of Hank's favorite movies. This man kept breaking down her walls without even knowing it. Those blue eyes were watching her intently and she felt her heart start to race even more. Taking one of the blankets, she made her way for the back seat when Rachel's arm across the door stopped her.

She leaned in close and whispered, "You should sit up front." Rachel looked over her shoulder to Scott. "He likes you."

"What?" Paige whispered harshly.

"Oh! And you like him." Turning to Scott and talking loudly, she said, "Scott, could you help Paige into the front seat? I need a minute to decompress."

Rachel grabbed the blanket from Paige's hand and hopped into the back of the truck.

"I'll remember this," Paige seethed through her clenched teeth, but Rachel's giggle made her smile.

Scott looked between the two women, but didn't say anything. He placed the blanket he held around her shoulders as a shiver shook her body. She wasn't sure if it was because she was wet or if it was because of his closeness and Rachel's words. She might be able to concede in her heart that he was a good guy. He just saved her from being taken, but she promised herself not to fall for anyone else again.

As they walked around the truck to the passenger side door, Scott placed his hand on the small of her back and leaned close. "That is the second time today someone was after you. How are you?"

Paige's heart was racing and her hold on her emotions was starting to slip, but the attempted kidnappings had nothing to do with her reaction. "I'm fine because of you." She held his gaze. "You saved me. Twice. Thank you."

Before she could do or say anything else, she climbed into the passenger seat and closed the door. Scott climbed into his side, but didn't start the engine.

"When we get back, we all need to be honest with each other." Scott looked at her, then Rachel. "Clearly there are people after either one or both of you."

"But..." Rachel started to protest from the back.

Scott sliced his hand through the air, halting her words. "I know, I know. You can take care of yourself and I'm sorry for not including you." Rachel crossed her arms, but remained silent. "I promise not to leave you out next time." He looked at Paige. "Together we can figure this out."

Paige nodded. It had been a long time since working together was something that she desired, but this felt good. For the first time in two years, she felt more like her old self. Not one lost in the darkness.

As they drove down the long drive, she spun scenarios in her mind as to why she would be targeted. The most obvious would be for her work, but the only people in New Freedom who knew what she actually did were Charles and Rachel. Neither of them would betray her.

Could someone have figured out where she went and come after her? Possibly.

Was it because Charles talked to her before they got to the hospital? She needed to figure out his message. Maybe Rachel could provide her with more answers. The only person besides the two in the truck with her that knew Charles even said anything was Marcus. She was certain that he didn't hear what Charles said and he never even asked about her conversation with Charles.

Marcus was a flirt, but she didn't see him as someone who would kidnap another person. Trying to figure this out on her own was starting to give her a headache. She was glad that she would have Scott and Rachel to help her figure it out. Because she wasn't sure next time she would be able to dodge whoever was coming for her.

Chapter 9

WATCHING THE SUV STOP beside the women brought back flashes of the black van that took Heather. The helplessness that paralyzed him back then tried to take over today, but his anger flared to life in time for him to react. The very thought of losing either of them wanted to steal the very breath from his lungs.

He couldn't let that happen. Rachel was his sister and he would always protect her despite her protests. Paige. She was an amazing woman. One that he would like to–who was he kidding? Women were a distraction, and as soon as she found out he was the reason someone was dead, she'd run in the opposite direction.

He said that they all needed to be honest with each other; maybe that included him as well. Paige deserved to know who she was working with.

They decided to have their conversation in the bunker because it was the most secure location on the property. The two women sat beside each other on the couch and Scott decided to stand behind one of the recliners. He was too energized to sit.

"Let's first start by reviewing what has happened in the last thirty-six hours." Buying himself more time to come clean.

Rachel chimes in. "Mom and Dad get run off the road."

"Your dad gave me the message, *'The sparrow has flown. Help Rachel find her. She can stop this.'*" Paige adds.

"Wait, Dad told you that? Why didn't you tell me?" Rachel sounded angry. This piqued his interest more.

"It's been a bit crazy around here." Paige pointed out. "I was going to tell you today when I got off of my shift."

Scott studied his sister, but she refused to look at him.

"Who is the sparrow, Rachel?" Scott needed her to talk. "Dad said you could find her."

She sighed. "The sparrow is Heather Zeits."

The air whooshed out of him and the weight of the past pressed around his chest like a vice grip. With each flash of memory, the crank twisted tighter.

"Who, exactly, is Heather Zeits?" Paige asked through the fog of memories.

"She is the girl who is dead because of me." Scott slammed his fist on the cushion of the recliner.

"You must consider yourself pretty important to cause such evil in the world," Rachel retorted. "You did not give the orders to kidnap Heather."

"No, but I was too distracted to even notice the van pull up to her." The twelve years of self doubt and pain seethed into his voice. "I should have been more aware of my surroundings."

"You were in love, big brother. No one, not even Dayton, blames you for what happened." Rachel stood and walked toward him. "You should stop punishing yourself for a crime you had nothing to do with."

Scott looked at Paige now that she knew the truth. He expected her to pull away or shun him for his role. Instead, he saw knowing in her eyes.

"The fault for the evil in this world lies solely with the evil ones who do the deeds." Paige's wise words wormed their way into his heart. He knew that they were true, but the doubt that he had carried with him for so long would be a hard layer to shed.

Rachel turned abruptly and stalked to the wall of screens. Typing quickly she started putting notes about what they discussed on the board. Under the phrase, "Crafton Accident" she wrote, "Sparrow=Heather Zeits."

Scott shook the thoughts of the past from his head and walked over to the conference table. Paige sat down and pointed to the chair beside her, suggesting that he take a seat. He sat next to her, expecting her to pull away like she had done last time, but she stayed where she was.

If he reached out, he could hold her hand. Nope. *Women are a distraction,* he reminded himself. Instead of dreaming about what it would be like to feel her petite hand in his, he should be focused on the conversation.

"So, Heather was taken how long ago? I feel like there is more to this story." Paige said.

Rachel opened her mouth to answer Paige, but Scott cut her off. "I will finish the story."

"Fine, but I'm still going to correct you when you get it wrong."

Scott huffed. "Twelve years ago, it was a week before I graduated high school. I had just been accepted into the wildland firefighter apprentice program and I wanted to celebrate with my girlfriend, Dayton Zeits."

For the first time in years, Scott let all of the memories wash over him. "We went to see a movie and get ice cream down at the Freezy Cone afterwards. Dayton's parents were away for the weekend and she was supposed to watch Heather. We took her with us even though all she wanted to do was stay at home alone. I didn't mind if she tagged along. I had everything I wanted back then. A girl that I loved. The job I had dreamed about."

Scott paused to regain control of the mess of emotions rolling through him. "We went to the park with our treats. It was dark but Dayton and I wanted to swing and I was hoping she would find a dark corner where we could pretend to be alone."

Scott looked straight ahead. "I didn't even notice the van that pulled up and Heather being taken until the door slammed and the vehicle pulled away."

Paige laid her hand on his arm. "Scott, this isn't your fault."

Scott locked gazes with her. "Don't you see? If I wouldn't have been distracted by a woman and paying attention to my surroundings like my father had trained me to do, then Heather would have never been taken."

Scott's chest heaved up and down. Paige didn't even blink at his outburst, but held his stare. With just her eyes, she quashed the anger that burned deep within.

Feeling more in control, Scott turned to Rachel. "I went to Dad and begged him to help us find Heather. He told me he couldn't. I accused him of only using his skills for those that could pay for him and whatever happened to 'using your skills to help people'." Scott blinked back tears. He refused to cry about the past. "He left that night for another mission, even missed my graduation."

He turned back to Paige. "I left for California the day after graduation and never spoke to him again until yesterday on the phone after their car crashed."

Paige pulled her eyebrows together. "What exactly did your father do for Uncle Sam?"

She hadn't pulled back after his own story. Maybe she would be able to handle his family's past as well.

He took a deep breath and continued. "Before my parents met, he worked for the intelligence community. He never told me what exactly he did, but the story goes that when he married my mother, whom he met on one of his missions, he switched to the private sector. He worked for some company that helped people in dire situations. He was the best at finding people. Even the ones the FBI or any other international agency couldn't find."

"It sounds like he was doing good work." Paige shifted toward him.

"I was proud of the work he did, until I realized that he only did it for the rich." He scoffed as the pain of the past resurfaced. "Evil doesn't care about your socioeconomic status."

"In fact, those with lower economic status tend to go missing more frequently than those of a higher status,"

Rachel stated matter-of-factly. "It's why Dad has dedicated all of his spare time the last twelve years to find Heather."

"They declared her dead seven years ago. Buried an empty casket. I visited her grave every time I was on leave." The dam holding his tears at bay was threatening to break.

He took a steadying breath. *Control your emotions. Focus on the task at hand.*

Rachel's voice was calm. "Dad wanted to find proof to bring closure to Mark and Shirley. Four days ago, he said that he found something that he wanted to run down. It's why he and Mom were traveling."

She typed "possible lead" under Heather's name on the screen.

What had his dad found? The questions he needed to ask his father were mounting. Scott asked a silent prayer that his dad would come out of his coma soon so they could get some answers.

"What else has happened?" Rachel refocused the group.

"I'm not sure if it is connected, but Mateo Cruz was hit over the head at the fire last night," Scott added. "I want to go talk with him today to see if he remembers anything. I know that the police will have to interview him once Tucker files his report, but I'm hoping that he will tell us as well."

"I will go with you." Paige got up. "Mateo doesn't know you very well and might be willing to open up more with me there."

"We can go once we are done here." Scott tugged her back to her seat. The feel of her hand in his gave him a calm after wading through the past. Once she sat, he let her hand go, but secretly he wanted to hold on.

"Finally, we had the abduction attempt of Paige," Rachel stated

"We don't know if they were after you or me," she protested.

"The taser stayed pointed at you when you pushed me away." Rachel quipped. "They were after you. The question is why?"

Paige sighed. "I was trying to wrack my brain on the way here. I could only think of two things. My job or the fact that Charles gave me a message yesterday."

"Can you give us the PR version of your job?" Scott asked.

Paige leaned forward, placing her forearms on the table, "I work for the DOD in RAD."

"That's not all that helpful, but we can assume whatever you are working on is desired by men wanting to do not so good things."

"Yes. I am supposed to meet the DCIS agent assigned to oversee my safety later today. I can ask him if there is any chatter."

Scott didn't like not knowing details. Details kept you alive, but he could also respect security clearance. She was probably going to shoot him down, but he had to at least mention the most logical security question.

"Until we know why someone is trying to abduct you, you shouldn't go places alone." Scott crossed his arms ready to push her on this. There was no way he was letting go alone.

"I would feel better if you let Scott be close by," Rachel spoke up. "Dad always said it is—

'Better to have back up and not need it than need back up and it's too far away.'" Scott and Rachel recited together.

Paige sat back in her chair. "Fine, but make sure you are not seen."

"Understood." Scott nodded as relief swept through him.

Rachel walked over to the supply closet that housed the gear. She punched in a code to unlock the door. That was new.

"Dad made some improvements when he semi-retired," Rachel said over her shoulder.

The room was the same size as the two bunkrooms, but the three walls were covered in shelves locked by a code. The shelves were backlit with blue LED lights that motioned to white when Rachel unlocked the first one.

"Along the east wall you have optics and small weapons. The north wall is where you will find coms and other electronic devices developed by yours truly. The west wall is where you will find larger weapons and tactical gear."

Scott gave a low whistle. "I'm not going to ask how he came to own all of this."

Paige whispered her astonishment. "Woah. Hank would have loved to see this."

It was like an operator's toy store. "Rachel, can you have a set of tactical gear and binocs for me as well as coms for both of us?"

When Rachel nodded, Scott turned to leave the room with Paige close behind him.

"Do you think the coms are necessary?"

"It will be easier to protect you if I can see and hear what is going on."

Paige didn't protest any further as they climbed the stairs back to the cabin.

"Do you mind if, after we talk with Mateo, we stop and get my car? I'm going to need it to get back and forth to town."

"It would be good for you to have a vehicle to meet your contact. I will go early to get into position."

"See but not be seen," she said with a wink.

"Exactly." This woman had a depth to her that he wanted to explore. She had the mind of an operative, but the heart of a healer. The fact that she lost so many people close to her and yet still was jumping in to help people said everything he needed to know about her character. For now, though, he needed to focus on why someone was trying to grab her.

Chapter 10

P AIGE'S NERVES HUMMED AS her mind tried to make sense of everything that Mateo had told them. Heather was stuck in a dark world. What did Heather Zeits know that warranted this much trouble? She took a look at Scott. He hadn't said much since they left Mateo's place.

"Care to share?"

Scott looked at her for a moment before returning his gaze to the road. "I'm still processing the fact that Heather Zeits is still alive. Part of me hopes we can reunite her with her family, but the operator in me knows the hell she must have gone through for twelve years."

Silence filled the space.

"I wonder how much of Heather actually still exists," he finally said in a hoarse whisper. "Twelve years is a long time to be in captivity."

Paige knew she needed to pull away from this man, but he was clearly in emotional pain so she reached out to him. She placed her hand gently on his shoulder.

"Let's find her first, then we can worry about getting her the help she needs."

His shoulder relaxed under her touch, and she felt some of the knots in her stomach unravel as well. She never dreamed that she would find herself in the middle of this kind of chaos when she moved here from DC.

Scott cleared his throat. "Tell me about the agent you're meeting with."

Clearly they were done talking about Heather for the moment, but she understood that.

When she didn't respond he continued to ask questions, "Height? Build? Does he have a limp? Anything to help me notice if anything is amiss?"

She spent the remainder of the car ride describing Agent Rollands to Scott. "Rachel told me that Rollands and your dad go way back and that's why he asked your dad to keep an eye on me while I was here."

"Wait, what?" Scott gripped the steering wheel tighter. "You didn't tell me you were in danger before you moved here."

"Calm down. The technology I'm working on is highly classified and Rollands wanted to make sure I was protected no matter where I went." She blew out a breath. "The lab I used to work at in DC had a state-of-the-art security system and I lived in their on-campus housing. He was more worried about protecting the project than me."

"I see. Well, hopefully he gives you a good update. Do you normally meet in person?"

Paige became restless. "We hardly ever meet in person. It's usually a secure conference call. In fact, this is only the third time I've met him in person since I moved out here, and the first two times, I requested equipment that he delivered personally so that there was no record of shipment to me."

Giving voice to that train of thought made the knot in her stomach return and caused her to squirm. Something was definitely off. She just hoped that whatever it was didn't bring death and destruction to this town, and in particular, the Craftons.

"Hey." Scott touched her knee. "I will be there. You don't have to worry."

The warmth of his touch was making it hard to think. She blinked to refocus. "I'm not worried about me. I'm worried about death following me here and destroying the little bit of happiness that I was able to find."

Scott squeezed her knee before letting her go. "God will be with us."

"Will He, though? He wasn't with anyone else who was important to me. They all died."

A single tear slipped down her cheek. She swiped at it. She really needed to stop crying in this man's presence. She was tougher than this.

"A wise woman once said, 'The fault for the evil of this world lies solely with the evil ones that do the deeds.' God did not promise us to never have evil things happen to us, but He came to bring us back to him. This world is broken because of sin. He sacrificed Himself so that one day we will be with Him, not so that nothing bad would ever happen to us on this earth."

Paige snorted. The answer seemed so simple, but so complicated.

"I know. It's clearly a truth that I struggle with sometimes too. When I have those moments of doubt, it gives me peace that one day there will be no more pain. No more evil."

"It's hard to wrap my mind around that given everything that I have seen."

Scott didn't push the subject any more and silence filled the space between them. It wasn't awkward or suffocating, but almost peaceful. She wasn't sure what it was about this man, but he made her want to not be alone anymore. To actually let someone see the whole Paige. The one that had been drifting away in the sea of grief.

After retrieving her car, Scott insisted that he follow her to her camper. She wanted to protest, but because of the events of the day, it was nice to have someone there.

She got out of her car and walked back to his truck as he got out. "Thanks for following me here."

"You're welcome. Nice digs." Scott nodded toward her retro style camper that was white on top and teal around the bottom. It had the rounded ends befitting of its nod to the past. It reminded her of her grandmother's 1963 camper that they went camping in every summer.

"I bought it off a Marine I had served with once, whose wife wanted a bigger one for their growing family. Móraí used to own an original one that was white and teal like this one. When I saw it, I knew that it was meant for me."

Paige had put a set of Adirondack chairs under the small awning where she and Rachel had sat some evenings just to talk. The inside was cozy, but she didn't need much space.

The dining table she used as her desk and she usually ended up eating outside on days when it wasn't too cold.

"It fits you."

She wasn't sure if she should accept that as a complement or be offended. Raising one eyebrow, she faced him.

Scott put his hands in the air. "Calm down. I only meant that it seems fun and it has its own style."

"Well, I am fun, or I used to be."

"Maybe one day I'll get to experience that fun side in full force."

She smiled. "I would like that."

As she watched him back away, Paige wondered what that would look like. To have a day of abandon. Not worrying about deadlines or being dragged down by the past. It sounded like a fantasy.

At 1430 she drove over to the cabin, even though she preferred to walk, only to find Scott leaning against the porch railing. He had changed into black cargo pants and a matching shirt that pulled across his chest.

She had seen him in street clothes and his fire chief uniform, but this version of Scott made her swoon. This man looked deliciously dangerous and her love-starved heart took off at the sight of him. For a brief moment, she let herself dream about what it would be like to be surrounded by his arms. Cherished. Protected.

Then the memory of Hank walking away for his last mission flashed in her mind.

Alone was better. They could be friends, but she couldn't let her heart run away with her good sense.

She got out of her car.

"You ready to go?" She stood at the foot of the steps.

Scott studied her for a moment, then descended the steps to stand right in front of her. She knew she should move, but her feet weren't listening.

His dark clothes drew out the gray in his eyes. Paige could get lost in these eyes. Her breath hitched as his gaze drifted to her lips, but before she could give into desire, he took a step back.

"We should get going. I want to be in position before he has a chance to get there."

Paige nodded. What had just happened? Maybe she could analyze it tonight while avoiding sleep. Or maybe it would invade her sleep, which made sleep almost tempting enough to chance the nightmares.

"I'll park at the Jumping Bean and wait until he arrives. He will probably be early." She started to walk towards her car, but he tugged on her arm.

He opened his palm to reveal an ear piece. "So we can communicate."

She put the piece into her ear. "Is there a way to turn it off?" She hated to ask, but clearance was strict. "It's not that I don't trust you, it's just that you haven't been cleared to be read in."

"Rachel showed me how to control it from my phone since she wanted to go back to the hospital." Scott flexed his jaw before huffing out a breath.

"Your mom and dad will pull through."

Scott tilted his head to the side with a slow half smile. "I've been praying to that end."

Maybe God heard Scott's prayers, but her prayers must not ever make it to His ears.

"We should go." She walked toward her car without looking back at him.

As she grabbed her door handle, an arm reached around her. Paige spun and brought the palm of her left hand around to strike her attacker. His arm swept her blow to the side while pinning her to him.

"Whoa. Paige, I was only trying to get your door." His voice lowered. "I won't let anything happen to you."

She needed to get her head in the game. When she felt the presence behind her and saw the arm, her instincts took over. She knew that she was safe with the Craftons, at least physically.

Now that her logical side of her brain caught up with her survival side, she noticed that she had found her way into Scott's arms. It was not how she envisioned this happening, but the feel of his toned body against hers sent a wave of yearning through her.

"Sorry, Scott." She pushed herself away. "I'm still a bit on edge from earlier."

"No worries." A slow smile crept across his face. "I enjoy being kept on my toes."

Without a doubt this man was a danger to her heart.

Refusing to break eye contact, he reached around her and opened her door. When he drew back they were inches from each other.

"We should probably get going," she whispered.

A deep throated, "Hmm" was his only response.

He stepped away this time. From both of their reactions today, she needed to keep her space. Otherwise, he would meet a tragic end. Something she didn't want to be responsible for.

Paige parked her car in front of the Jumping Bean as Scott kept driving toward the park.

She doubted that Rollands was there already, but given that Scott was in tactical gear and now a public figure, it was best if he stayed out of sight from as many people as possible.

He wasn't carrying an automatic weapon, but he looked the part of a highly trained soldier or scary bad guy. Given the suspicions that the previous chief's life ended in, it was best for him to continue to be the prodigal hero soldier returned home. She didn't want to be the cause of any trouble for him.

Paige got out of her car and ordered her favorite drink, a cold brew with vanilla cream foam. She usually only treated herself to the nitro brew when she was pulling an extended shift. Since she didn't get her normal post shift rest, the caffeine was necessary.

She found a corner table where she could watch the door and the rest of the small cafe.

Scott's voice burst through the coms and made her jump. "I'm in position."

"Copy that, Flyboy."

"I guess that makes you Devil Doc." She could hear the smile in his voice.

She smirked. "The unit called me Doc. Hank told them I looked too much like an angel to be called a devil."

"I would have to agree with Hank."

Focus on the mission. She cleared her throat. "Remember, when I tuck my hair behind my ear, you need to cut the coms."

"I got you, Doc. Just enjoy your coffee. I'll let you know when he arrives."

She tried to relax and enjoy the soft jazz music playing over the speakers. She usually enjoyed people watching, but today her mind didn't want to stay in the moment.

A man in an expensive looking suit and bright red tie, strode through the door. Stanley Fox. She had to resist the urge to approach him and ask him what he was going to do to help poor Mrs. Miller. As if sensing he was being watched, Stanley slowly turned toward her. One side of his lips lifted as he nodded in her direction.

The man screamed power, from his attire to the way he commanded the room as he walked toward her. What could he possibly want?

"You must be Paige." His smooth voice only grated on her nerves.

Scott remained quiet which she was thankful for.

"I am. And you are Stanley Fox. Real Estate tycoon, the town's golden boy, and all around good guy." She put as much sarcasm into her voice as she could muster.

"Marcus said you had a snarky sense of humor."

As if summoning him with the mere mention of his name, Marcus walked through the door. His gaze swept the small cafe as if looking for someone. When he saw Stanley talking with her, shock then anger seared in his eyes before he reeled in his reaction.

"Speaking of Marcus," she dipped her head toward the door. "He just arrived. I'll let you two besties have your coffee date."

She pushed past Stanley and sent a long hard stare at Marcus. What else had he told his friends about her? And more importantly, why was he friends with Stanley Fox? Besides the appreciation of self, they didn't seem like they had a bunch in common.

"What is your location?" Scott's hushed voice grounded her to the moment. She put her phone to her ear so that she didn't draw attention to herself for talking with someone that wasn't there.

"I'm taking a walk towards the Freezy Cone."

"Please be vigilant. We don't know who is after you."

"I will. I just needed to get out of there. Stanley Fox sets me on edge." She shuddered and increased her pace.

"Most people think he's a good guy. His company bought the land that he then donated to the town to expand the park."

"On paper, a sly man can look like an angel, but there is something in his eyes that isn't quite right."

"Never looked into the man's eyes," Scott quipped.

"Very funny, Flyboy." His antics helped her shake off that strange encounter.

"Rollands is approaching the bench." Scott's harsh whisper brought her the rest of the way into focus.

"I'm going to make my way over there."

"Paige, I think there is something wrong. He just shook his head as if to try and clear it."

Paige picked up speed. "Don't approach him, I'm almost there."

"He reached into his pocket and it looks like he is writing something. This isn't the best angle."

Paige started to jog when she got to the parking lot. She was 100 yards away. As soon as she stepped foot onto the play area, she caught sight of him.

"I have a visual."

In slow motion, Rollands leaned back against the bench and looked toward the sky. Paige broke out in an all out run. "Call 911. I need an ambulance now."

Within seconds she was at Rollands' side.

"Agent Rollands." She lowered him to the ground and placed her fingers on his wrist. His chest was not moving and she couldn't find a radial pulse. Moving to his neck to check his carotid for a pulse, she whispered, "Don't take another good man, God."

"Amen."

"That wasn't exactly a prayer," she gritted out as she began compressions on Rollands. Scott appeared at her side and pulled out a barrier from his side pocket.

"You wouldn't happen to have an AED in there?" she quipped.

Scott cocked his eyebrow at her, but said nothing. Professional mode. Right.

After thirty compressions, she paused to let Scott give Rollands two breaths. She could hear the sirens coming.

"Come on Rollands. You've got to tell me your message."

They continued with rounds of compressions until Hudson and Stevens arrived with an AED and took over CPR.

Scott pulled her to the side. "I know you can help them, but let them do their job now. We can meet them at the hospital."

Paige nodded her head because she didn't trust her voice to work without breaking the emotional dam within. A business card laid on the bench. Before they walked away, she reached down and tucked it in her pocket.

"Where is your truck?"

"It's parked on the other side of the trees."

"My car is still at the Jumping Bean."

"Your car is closer. Care for a run?"

Paige wasn't sure she could even walk to her vehicle, but Scott tugged on her hand. They fell into sync with one another as Scott yelled for people to get out of their way.

Once they got to her car, Paige tossed Scott her keys. "You drive."

Without a word, he slipped into the driver's seat and waited for her to buckle in. Scott pulled into the ambulance bay at the ER minutes later. As the fire chief, she suspected that people would be more forgiving of him taking one of the spaces than an off-duty paramedic.

They rushed into the side of the ER and spotted the room where they took Rollands. Nurses and techs wove in and out of the room as a doctor shouted orders. They stood out of the way as Scott held her to his side. When the commotion slowed and silence settled over the staff, Paige knew that Rollands' message died with him.

She couldn't hold back the flood any longer. Turning into Scott's chest, she let the sobs wrack her body. Inside his embrace she felt safe, but she needed to chin up and face reality. Rollands died trying to give her a message.

Paige pushed back from Scott and took him by the hand. "We need to find a quiet spot."

"I know just the place." Scott tugged her down the hall until they stood in front of the hospital's chapel.

She felt like a fraud for seeking quiet in a place that was meant to worship God since she and Him weren't on the best of terms right now.

"You may not want to speak with Him, but He's still here with you."

Paige snorted. "Then why is Rollands dead? Where was God?"

Scott said nothing but simply looked at her with peace in his eyes. God's peace. How she longed to feel that peace again, but all she felt was isolation.

"And whose fault is that? God is with you always, all you have to do is let Him in." Móraí's voice filled her mind this time.

Paige squeezed her eyes shut and collapsed into the back pew. She laid her head on the hard, worn surface of the pew in front of her.

A few seconds later, the pew in front of her shifted slightly and a hand started rubbing her back. Scott's spicy scent tickled her nose and brought her a measure of comfort.

"Thanks." Paige sat up and wiped away the remnants of her tears.

"I'm here when you want to talk about it."

Paige wanted to ask him her questions. Tell him her worst fears, but that meant he would end up like everyone else she let get too close to her. She couldn't be the reason that this handsome man died. The fear pulsed through her veins at the thought.

"You and your family should stay away from me, I am a death wish." Paige fled the chapel, hoping to put enough distance between the two of them to keep him safe.

Chapter 11

I T TOOK HIS BRAIN a few moments to register what exactly happened.

"Paige, wait!" He ran after her praising God that his long strides caught up with her quickly. "Paige, please." He pulled on her arm to turn her around.

"You should stay far away from me." She pushed away from him. "Everyone that cares about me dies." Her chin started to quiver. "I don't want you or your sister to be next."

"We can't stop death from coming. We can only live this life with purpose, and I believe that God brought the two of us together." Realizing what that sounded like, he quickly added, "to help figure out what is going on."

He waited for her to respond, but she said nothing. Thoughts were swirling behind those gorgeous green eyes. He prayed she didn't run away. She started to make him reconsider his strict no-woman in his life rule.

"Please, Paige. I need you. Rachel needs you. We can't figure this out without you."

"That's not true. You and Rachel are two of the most capable people I've met, but I appreciate the sentiment."

She blew out a breath and he held his. "I'll stay, but I want it on the record that I warned you of your fate."

The corners of his mouth lifted. "I have been so warned."

She reached into her back pocket and pulled out a business card. "Rollands dropped this on the bench. It's safe to assume that this is the note you saw him write while sitting there."

Scott took the business card. The front showed him that it was one of Agent Rollands' cards and on the back was one word Ghostcode.

Scott scrunched his eyebrows. "Does that mean anything to you?"

"I think he was trying to warn me about a Ghostcode in my program." She puckered as if the very thought left a sour taste in her mouth.

"I'm assuming that's a bad thing."

"It could be nothing, but it could be everything." She started to pace in front of him.

"You're debating what you can tell me." It wasn't a question. He knew that clearance was something he may or may not have, and until she checked in with someone in DC, he would respect that boundary.

"You don't have to tell me about your work. I get it. Is there anyone here in New Freedom that has the clearance to help you? That is, if you need help."

She looked up at him with relief. "Rachel and Charles were the only two read in on my research in case something happened to me. They knew who to contact and/or how to destroy it if necessary."

He was liking this research less and less. His mind was starting to run wild with what she could possibly be creating. "Since we are here, let's go get Rachel so she can help you."

She hesitated but then nodded her head.

Scott had to resist the urge to place his hand on her back as they walked out of the ER.

"Paige McFarland? Chief Crafton?"

Scott's spine stiffened. Who could need them now? Slowly, he turned.

Officer Turvet walked toward them briskly. The rumor was that Harry was going to take his detective's exam and be Detective O'Connor's replacement upon his retirement in the fall. "Do you have a moment to give statements about this afternoon?" Turvet pulled out a pad and pen.

"Of course." A man died under unusual circumstances. The police were going to have to investigate. He just hoped that they gave this case more energy than they had given Heather's.

Trina stood behind the nurse's station. "You all can use the conference room down the hall for some privacy and quiet."

Turvet asked Scott to go first, and then took Paige's statement. "So, let me get this right, you were supposed to meet Agent Rollands at 1600," he looked at Paige, "and you decided that you needed to be there as backup?" He sent Scott a questioning gaze.

Scott didn't want to tell him about the attempted kidnapping because Paige said she didn't want to report it. He looked at Paige, letting her know that it was her call how much to tell Turvet.

She blew out a breath. "Might as well tell you since Rollands is dead. Earlier today, two men in a black SUV tried to abduct me. Scott prevented it from happening."

The look of admiration in her eyes just about undid him. *Keep your head in the mission.*

"Do you have any idea if the two things are related?" Turvet asked.

"Next time the goons show up to abduct me, I'll ask them what it's all about and then we'll know if they are related," Paige snapped.

Scott fought a smirk. "I think Paige is trying to say that until we know a bit more, it's hard to say if the two events are related."

Turvet studied them both for a moment. "I will let you know if we find anything in our investigation that would connect the two, but given that we don't know what Agent Rollands came to tell you, we should proceed with caution."

Again Scott deferred to Paige. If she wanted to mention the note, then he would let her.

"Thank you, Officer Turvet. Do you mind if we go and visit Mr. and Mrs. Crafton now?"

"I will keep you posted on the investigation." He put the pad and pen back in his pocket. "I may need to ask you some follow up questions."

"Of course." Paige turned and left. Scott followed her in silence.

Once the elevator doors closed, Paige crossed her arms in front of her. "You know that DCIS is going to come and take over this investigation right?"

"Makes sense since Rollands worked for them."

She sighed heavily. "I'm going to have to report the attempted abduction. I was going to tell Rollands today about it."

"Until they get here, we will keep you safe."

"Thanks, Scott."

He wanted to say more. To ask her about her thoughts. Help her process everything, but the doors opened to the ICU floor and the moment was lost.

With everything that happened with Rollands, Scott hadn't had a chance to check in with Rachel about either of his parents. He had to figure out what was going on while also protecting Paige. Could her abduction be connected to Heather Zeits? It was highly unlikely. The most logical possibility was that someone was after her research, but who?

As they came around the nurses station, Scott nodded towards Tylan. Maybe he should bring in his friend. He was a PI, and a good one according to his mother. Before he could ask Tylan anything, Rachel came out of their father's room.

"Is he awake?" Scott asked.

Rachel came up short. "He is in and out. They have him on heavy pain medicine so his consciousness isn't with clear thinking. The doctor said that if he makes it the next twenty-four hours without a setback, he should be able to make a full recovery." She pinned him with her eyes. "But it's going to be a long recovery. I hope you plan on sticking around to help us."

Scott pulled her into a hug. "I promise."

He knew that Rachel didn't like people giving her hugs that she didn't initiate, but she seemed to relax after a moment.

She pulled back and looked at Rachel. "What happened?"

Scott motioned for Tylan to come over. "Could you go with these two to a conference room so that they can talk? I'm going to visit with Mom and Dad before we head out."

Tylan said no words, but acknowledged him with a slight nod.

"Paige, you can trust Tylan as much as you can trust me with information. He can also help us."

Uncertainty warred in her green eyes. She glanced at Rachel who backed his invitation.

"Tylan is the best PI, and he is one of the only other people in town who knows about our family in depth."

Those words seemed to win her over. "It might be a good thing to have a fresh set of eyes on this situation."

Scott watched the trio enter the conference room located right next to the staff entrance doors. He took a deep breath and let it out slowly. He stepped through the curtain of his father's room. The man looked much the same as he did last time except with a few less IV lines running.

"Hey Dad," Scott choked out.

The man in the bed stirred and then groaned.

"Don't move, Dad. It's me, Scott. You are in the hospital."

"Scott?" Charles opened his eyes almost the whole way. "Did your mother survive?"

Tears started to gather in Charles' eyes. He blinked them away. Scott had never seen his dad cry. Ever. He was going to chalk it up to the medicine and the fragile state he was in due to his injuries.

"Mom is awake. I'm going to see her next."

"Good, good." Dad drifted back to a medicated slumber.

"Sleep well, Dad." Scott patted his leg. He hadn't realized how much tension he carried not knowing if his father would ever wake up again. Just this short conversation lifted a huge weight off his shoulders.

Scott stepped out of the room and checked the hallway for Paige, Rachel, and Tylan. They were still in the conference room. He could see Tylan standing so that he was facing both into the room and keeping an eye on the hall through the large window. Tylan was a good man and would keep the women safe.

Scott knocked softly on his mother's door and heard a quiet, "Come in."

He braced himself as he stepped into the room. There sat his mother in lounge pants and one of his dad's shirts. She was reading a book that she quickly put on the nightstand beside her.

"Scott. I'm so glad that you came." She attempted to stand, but did so too quickly and swayed. In two long strides, he caught her by the elbow and helped her sit back down.

"You need to stay seated and you really shouldn't be reading." He pointed to her book.

"I know my limits perfectly well, but I appreciate your concern." She patted his hand. "Now give your mom a hug."

The smells of disinfectant were pushed away when his mom wrapped her arms around him. He breathed in the familiar scent of her soap. It was a mixture of lavender and lemon.

"You scared us there, Mom."

She swatted at his shoulder when he took a step back.

"It'll take more than that to kill me. When I figure out who sent them..." Paola's nostrils flared.

"Calm down, Mom. Rachel, Paige, and I have been working together to figure out who did this to you." He knew this next question might not go over well, but he needed to know. Mom, do you know anything about what Dad has been up to lately?"

"I don't like your tone. What have you found out?"

"Mom, please answer the question."

She massaged her head as if a headache was roaring to life. She sighed heavily. "I told him to call you so many times, but you both are stubborn men." She smiled softly. "Who have the biggest hearts."

She patted the bed next to where she sat. "Sit." She waited until he sat before she continued. "What you said to him when you left made him take a long, hard look at himself."

"It wasn't my most shining moment," Scott admitted with a wince.

"True, but the words came from the heart. And they were words your father needed to hear. That assignment was his last. As soon as he returned, he walked away from the company. Mostly. Ever so often they ask him to help find someone, but he does it from here and only the cases he wants to take."

"So what does he do now? I don't see Dad going fishing to fill his spare time."

"He started an organization to help those who are lost. He didn't want what happened to the Zeits to happen to anyone else. Rachel can show you everything when you go back to the bunker. That became their headquarters."

"Rachel refuses to tell me because she said Dad wanted to tell me."

"Send Rachel in before you leave and I will make sure she tells you everything. Charles will understand." His mom patted his cheek. "It is good to have you home, son."

"It's good to be home, Mom." For the first time in twelve years, he meant those words. New Freedom was his home. He would do what he could to make sure it was a safe place to be.

Scott walked down the hall to get Rachel and Paige. As he reached the door, it opened and the last of the conversation flowed out.

"Let me call in Ronnie to stand guard, and then I'll meet you at the cabin."

"Thank you for helping us, Tylan." Scott's words made Tylan stop short.

"You are some of the only family I have. I will do what I can to bring down this evil. New Freedom is our home and I need to keep it safe for Sari."

Scott pulled into the cabin lane. He had dropped Paige off to retrieve her car and Rachel opted to go with her. He had agreed only because he would be following them the whole way home. This also gave him time to think about the organization that his father started. How big of an operation did he have? How did he find clients? Who was all involved in the town?

His phone rang and Scott picked it up through the Bluetooth in his truck.

"Crafton."

"Chief, it's Tucker."

Scott wasn't on duty until 0700 tomorrow. Whatever Tucker was calling about must be important.

"Go ahead."

"We just got the report back from the state fire investigator about the Miller fire."

"That was fast."

"Apparently, this fire matches two other fires to the south of us that the state had already investigated. They are waiting for the chemical test to return from the lab, but the burn patterns and property situation match. All the properties were sitting vacant either waiting to be put on the market or stuck in probate."

"The arsonist is smart to target homes that have no one necessarily looking after them." Were they watching places or did they have some kind of insider knowledge of different properties?

"Makes you wonder what was happening in them before they were burnt to the ground." Tucker brought up another valid point.

"Thanks for the update, Tucker." His next words were cut off by the alarm at the fire station. The emergency alert system triggered on his phone, displaying the location of the fire. Even though it was his day off, he kept the alert system turned on. It allowed him to keep a pulse on the company and community.

The address on the truck's screen made his blood run cold. The Zeits' house.

"I'll meet you there."

"Chief, we can handle this."

"I know you can, but this one is personal." Scott squeezed the wheel. "I won't gear up unless you need me to."

"I'll see you there."

Tucker was a few years older than him. Scott didn't remember much about Tucker growing up, but he was loyal and dedicated to the company and this community. That was all Scott needed to know about him.

Scott pulled next to Paige's car and put down the window. Paige leaned on the door. "What's wrong?"

"You and Rachel go ahead and start without me." He pointed towards the cabin. "Tylan should be here soon to help out too. There is a fire at the Zeits' house."

"I'm not on duty, but I can go if you need help."

"No, I would feel better if you were both here to protect each other."

Respect shown in her green eyes as she gave him a quick nod. "Be safe, Flyboy."

"Always, Doc."

On his way to the fire, Scott called Tylan.

"Jamison."

"Tylan, it's Scott. The Zeits' house is on fire. I'm going to check it out. Paige and Rachel are in the bunker. I'll meet you there when the fire is out."

"Understood. What are the chances that the Zeits' house catches fire when we start looking for Heather again?" Tylan gave voice to his very thoughts.

"That's why I'm headed over there. I'll update you guys when I get back."

Scott arrived at the scene a few minutes later. He took in the crew and how they worked efficiently. Tucker was by Engine One, listening to the radio chatter and giving orders to the men outside. Scott had only been chief for a few days, but the company he inherited was well trained. Tucker was a natural at leading the team. If he was to believe the rumors, Tucker didn't even put in for the chief position.

Scott stood a safe distance away. Theories of what this fire meant in light of what they learned over the last two days played in his head. Why would someone set the Zeits' home on fire? If you asked any of the Zeits, they would say that Heather was dead.

This didn't make sense, but he felt like he needed to be here. He might see something while the others took care of the fire.

The fire was mostly under control when he noticed movement in the neighbor's yard. Without drawing attention to himself, Scott made his way towards the fence gate. Thankful for the noise of the fire and crew, Scott eased the handle open and stepped into the yard.

He couldn't see their face, but by the shape of their build he was safely guessing this was a woman. Could it be the arsonist? Although it's not as common, there had been documented cases of female arsonists. In most of those cases though, they were seeking attention and this woman was hiding and watching. An odd behavior.

"Are you alright, miss?" Scott called out.

She snapped her head towards him. When recognition hit her eyes, she gave a small gasp.

"Heather?" Scott said breathlessly.

Hardness filled her eyes. "I did what I could. Charles needs to figure the rest of it out."

Without another word, she took off running. She jumped the back fence in a blink of an eye and dashed around the next house. It took Scott a moment to jump into action. He heard a motorcycle rev to life before he got over the fence. Coming around the house, he saw her taillights fade into the distance.

Heather Zeits was alive and she was in New Freedom.

Chapter 12

P AIGE KNEW SHE NEEDED to call in what happened. It would be better if it came from her than from the police in New Freedom.

Pushing out a breath, Paige tried to focus her mind. "You don't happen to have a secure line here in the bunker, do you?"

Rachel gave her a smirk. "Of course. Dad loved old spy movies. I think they made him laugh at the inaccuracy of it all." Rachel pointed to the corded red phone on the wall, and her comment now made sense.

"Classic. I need to call in before Tylan gets here so that I can speak freely." She hated the secrets and the red tape. In addition to checking in, she would also request security clearance for Scott.

"I'll go get us some computers so we can start searching when you finish."

Paige nodded her agreement and picked up the phone. She would call Rollands' supervisor first. Rollands made her memorize the number when she moved out here just in case she couldn't get a hold of him in an emergency.

"Hunter," the gruff voice barked across the line.

"Agent Hunter. This is Paige MacFarland. We have a situation."

"Tell me what happened." Keyboard keys clicked filling the space on the line while she gathered her thoughts. No place to start than at the beginning. She told Hunter about being followed, the attempted kidnapping, and then Agent Rollands' death.

The typing ceased when she told him the last part. "I'll send someone out to take over the investigation. Are you in a secure location?"

"Yes. Charles Crafton and his family have been keeping me safe over the last twenty-four hours."

"Charles Crafton. I haven't heard that name in years." Hunter sounded impressed. "You are in good hands. Is the program finished?"

She wanted to run a few more tests before she handed it back over for a larger scale test. Her reputation and career rode on the success of this project. Now with Rollands' note about the ghostcode, she needed to go over the whole program with a fine tooth comb to make sure there were no surprises when they released it into the world.

"I would like a few more days to finish my primary tests before handing it over." Not a full out lie, but not mentioning the note Rollands left her was risky.

"I'll give you forty-eight hours."

Two days was hardly enough time to go through the whole thing by herself. She would have to ask Rachel to help her, and even then it'll take the better part of twenty-four hours.

"One more thing, sir." She knew she was pushing her luck, but she had to ask. "I'm requesting security clearance for Scott Crafton. He is a part of my protection detail since Charles is still in the hospital."

"Crafton is in the hospital? Why hadn't you told me that?" Hunter roared.

"I meant no harm by it, sir. It was a car accident. His son, Scott, has been looking after me and saved me from being kidnapped."

Hunter said nothing for what felt like an eternity. After blowing out a breath, he agreed to run the security clearance check, but made no promises it would go through.

"Until he comes back cleared, you are to tell him nothing about the program."

"Understood, sir." This wasn't her first need-to-know mission, but she kept her biting retort to herself.

"I'll send Agent Wilson out on the next flight. He should be to you tomorrow. Stay safe, MacFarland."

"Will try my best, sir."

"What did Agent Hunter have to say about Scott?"

Paige spun around at Rachel's question. It was good she was looped in because Paige wasn't sure how long Rachel had been standing there.

"He is going to run the clearance, but said to keep it need-to-know until he gets back to me."

She sighed. Maybe it was time to leave government work. If she ever found someone, she'd never be able to tell him about anything at her job. Paige's eye widened slightly. Since when was she thinking about finding someone? Scott's face flashed in her mind. The handsome fireman

143

proved himself to be a good man, but that was the problem. Everyone she ended up caring for died.

"I'm sure he'll come back with high enough clearance."

Paige blinked. "Let's hope so. I don't like leaving him in the dark."

Rachel smirked. "I'm glad you like him. He's different, in a good way, than when he left."

"Well, the military will do that to a person." It was hard for her to remember what she was like before the military, before she lost everyone.

"So will loss." Rachel's voice was soft.

She wasn't sure if Rachel was talking about her or Scott. Maybe both. She had told Rachel that she had no family left and that most of her friends reenlisted and were scattered across the globe.

Paige cleared her throat pushing the emotion back down. She needed to focus. She only had forty-eight hours to check over every line of code in her program, looking for anything that didn't belong.

"We should get started. Hunter only gave me forty-eight hours before he wants the program back in DC."

Rachel's eyebrows shoot up. "I noticed you didn't mention the note that Agent Rollands gave you."

"It was either tell him and he demand me hand over the program to have others comb through it, or I do it myself so I know that nothing is wrong with it."

"Scott wanted me to help track down Heather Zeits. To pick up where my dad left off." Rachel nodded toward the computer monitors.

The security system dinged and showed Tylan at the front door of the cabin.

"I'll go get him." Rachel hopped out of her chair. "Maybe he can look for Heather. Then I can help you search the program."

Rachel was coming back into the bunker with Tylan in tow as Paige finished locking down her computer. She always worked in a bubble. This prevented hackers from attempting to steal her work. If her computer wasn't connected to a network, even her secure VPN, there was no way to see what you were doing unless you were looking at the physical computer.

Tylan took a seat across from her at the conference table. "Thanks for helping us, Tylan. Let me get you Dad's computer."

Tylan rose one eyebrow at Rachel. "Will Charles mind if I use his computer?"

Rachel looked torn.

"Rachel, go ahead and copy any files you think Tylan will need from your dad's computer. Then you can come and help me look through code." Paige hoped Tylan wouldn't ask more about what they were doing.

"Good idea." Rachel opened one of the drawers under the large monitor. Pulling out a USB drive, she opened up her father's computer. In a matter of minutes she handed the drive to Tylan.

"This is all I could find in his files. Hopefully it'll give you a good start."

"If the rumors are even half true about your father, then I'm sure this will be more than enough to get me started." Tylan opened his own laptop and plugged in the drive.

Paige pulled two chairs close together as Rachel brought over a second monitor.

"Good idea," they said at the same time.

Paige couldn't help the giggle that escaped. The situation was dire, but it felt good to let out a bit of happiness into the room. Tylan only looked at them briefly before returning to his laptop.

"Could I get another monitor? I left my extender at the office," he grumbled.

"Have computer envy, Tylan?" Rachel countered.

Tylan narrowed his eyes.

"Relax, Ty. I was only joking." She sighed.

"Since when did you start with the jokes?"

"Since I became friends with Paige." Rachel bowed her head slightly towards Paige. "She is the master of sarcasm and quick quips. I am her student."

Tylan shot her a curious look. Paige shrugged. "I do what I can to better those around me."

"See what I'm talking about? Master." She pointed at Paige, then turned her finger toward herself. "Student."

For the next hour, Paige and Rachel reviewed line after line of code while Tylan silently searched for any more clues about Heather. Paige enjoyed the silence.

When the phone in the middle of the table rang, Paige nearly jumped out of her seat.

Rachel hit the speaker button and spoke for all of them. "Scott, you're on speaker. Paige and Tylan are here."

"How is it going with the search?"

"Tylan is looking through Dad's files to find a clue. Paige and I are looking through computer code."

"So, I'm going to assume that no one has thought about food yet."

At the mention of food, Paige's stomach decided to protest its lack of nourishment.

"I could eat," Rachel stated.

"I'll pick up some Chinese and come down. I need to fill you all in on what we found at the fire, but food first."

"A man after my own heart." Paige wanted to grab the words out of the air. Tylan gave her a half smirk and Rachel bit her lip to keep from smiling.

Scott started to laugh, which only caused the blush on her neck to rise. "Well, if it were that simple, I would have offered food earlier."

"Don't get ahead of yourself, Flyboy. I warned you about my track record." Somberness settled over the room. *Smooth one, Doc,* she chided herself.

"You know my response. I'll keep praying until you realize its truth."

Nothing like having a deeply personal conversation with other people in the room. Of course, they had no idea what they were talking about. She needed to lighten the mood again.

"Hurry with that food or I'll get hangry."

"Hangry?" Scott questioned.

"Hungry Paige equals an angry Paige."

He chuckled. "Let's all be spared angry Paige."

Rachel snickered and Paige shot her a look. What was this? Gang up on Paige time? She really did need that food.

"No worries. I'll come to your rescue, Doc."

She knew that he said the words out of jest, but they slammed into her with the force of a semi. In that moment, she knew he would not just bring her food, but if she was in trouble, he would be there. She wasn't alone, and if she was honest with herself, she quite liked it. She had forgotten what it was like to be a part of a tight knit group.

Being alone kept her from the heartache of losing anyone else, but being alone left her without help and someone to care if she needed it. It was foolish to think that one never needed help. Look at her now. Someone was coming after her. Agent Rollands, the man supposed to be protecting her, was dead. If she needed to abandon her fear of being hurt, it was now.

"I know." She paused, hoping that he would get the deeper meaning. "Don't forget Hunan Chicken for me."

"The lady likes some spice. It fits you. Any other special requests?"

The others put in their orders while Paige went back to studying her code. Before she realized how much time had passed, Scott let himself into the bunker. The smell of fried food, soy sauce, and spice made her mouth water.

Her stomach growled in anticipation.

Scott chuckled. "Let's pray before Paige's stomach turns her into angry Paige."

The twinkle in his eye made her heart stutter. The man had no clue what he was doing to her resolve. Or maybe he did. Paige pushed that thought aside. He told her that women were a distraction. He wasn't flirting with her. He just wanted to be friends.

She turned off her computer and helped Rachel get plates for everyone. They each took their chosen food to one of the four stools around the kitchen island.

"Scott, I can't wait any longer," Rachel blurted out. "Tell us what you found at the fire."

"You were never very patient. Good to know some things haven't changed."

Rachel glared at Scott.

"Alright. As they were wrapping up the blaze I noticed movement in the yard of the next door neighbor." Scott took a bite of his food. Paige wasn't sure if he was stalling or not, but she wished he would tell them already.

"When I approached, I could see that it was a woman." He stared at his plate for a moment.

Paige felt the food harden in her stomach. Whoever Scott saw was a big deal.

He sighed. "It was Heather. She was standing right in front of me. Before running she told me, 'I did what I could. Charles has to figure out the rest.'"

He put down his fork and wiped his mouth on his napkin. "She was over the fence and on her motorcycle before I came out of the shock of seeing her in the flesh."

She wanted to reach out to him and hold his hand. Give him comfort, but held back.

He ran his fingers through his hair. "That's not the strangest thing though. Inside the house there were about ten different paintings stacked along the kitchen counters. The fire was set in the opposite side of the house. Most of them were unharmed by the water. It was like whoever set the fire wanted the art to burn last."

"That is weird." Tylan rubbed the stubble on his chin.

"Do either of you have contacts at the FBI?" Paige pointed her fork at Scott and then Tylan. "If the paintings are stolen, they would know." Paige stabbed another piece of chicken. "The FBI would also have the resources to tell us if the paintings are real or fake."

Rachel glared at Tylan.

"Fine." The man huffed. "I'll call my contact. He doesn't work in white collar, but he should be able to get me in touch with someone that does."

"Thanks, Tylan." Rachel said as if she would have given him any other choice.

It seemed that Tylan had a complicated relationship with the FBI. He was here helping them, she reminded herself. It was none of her business.

"We should get back at it." Paige tilted her head towards the computers.

"Agreed." Rachel collected everyone's plate and brought them over to the sink.

"I'll wash those. You go help Paige with the code." Scott took the washcloth from his sister.

"He brings food and washes dishes." Scott looked up from the sink with a grin on his face. Did she just say that out loud?

"I'm full of surprises." He winked at her before returning to the chore. Rachel put her hand over her mouth and cleared her throat. Paige could have sworn she saw a smile on her friend's face before she schooled her expression.

Paige and Rachel settled back into their chairs and started scrolling through code again. Scott joined Tylan when he finished the dishes. She caught him looking at them over her computer screen. The sight made her smile and tuck her chin.

"I think I found something." Rachel's words snapped Paige out of the silent conversation between her and Scott.

"Send it to my screen."

Rachel got out of her chair and leaned over Paige's shoulder. "There. Fifth line from the bottom of the screen."

Paige brought the line towards the top so she could see on both sides of the code.

"I've seen part of that code before." Rachel squinted at the screen as if doing so would make her remember where she saw it.

"Well, it's a good thing that we are working in a bubble because it looks like it is programmed to initiate the code only when connected," Paige said while staring at the rest of the code.

"What exactly are we looking at?"

Scott's voice in her ear made her jump.

Scott stood up straighter putting distance between them. "Sorry. I didn't mean to scare you."

"I wasn't expecting you to be so close." Paige turned off her screen. "Answer the next question honestly." She spun to face him. "Can you read computer code?"

"Not even if my life depended on it. I know my way around some tech, but programming was never my thing."

"Good enough." She turned the computer back on. "Sorry for the questions, but until your clearance comes back, I have to follow protocol."

"You asked to give me clearance?"

She looked over her shoulder. "Yes. I wanted to bring you on board. I trust you."

Emotions stormed in his eyes before he whispered, "Thanks, Paige."

"Now." She pointed at the lines of code on the screen. "These lines of code look like typical ghostcode."

Scott put his hand on her shoulder. "Stop right there. I've been meaning to ask, but half embarrassed about it. What exactly is a ghostcode?"

She patted his hand before he removed it. "A ghostcode is code in a program that does not affect the function of the program."

"So why put it in there if it's useless?"

"I never said it was useless. You can use them in the developmental stages to run calculations while the program is running. It allows us to gather data and make adjustments to the program."

"Makes sense." He nodded.

"This code is not one that I put in here."

"How can you remember all of the codes that you put in here? This program looks like it goes on forever."

"Valid question, but I never write my ghostcodes to send data over the internet, and this one is designed to take the calculations from all of the ghostcodes embedded in the program and send it to this IP address."

She wrote it down. "We finally have a lead."

"Why only take the calculations? Why not a copy of the whole program?"

"A program of this size would take quite a bit of bandwidth and would be easy to track, but the calculations would give enough information about all parts of the program in small separate files that wouldn't draw any unnecessary attention," Rachel stated matter-of-factly.

"That's what I was going to say. Great minds do think alike." Paige spun her chair to face Scott, who took a step back.

"Whoever this is only wants to see what the program is capable of—not necessarily reproduce it. In other words, they want to be able to prepare to outsmart it."

"I'm going to pretend that that made sense, even though I have no idea what the program actually does."

"Trust me." Paige stood even though she only came to his shoulders. It was better than sitting. "There are plenty of not-so-good guys that would want to get ahead of this technology."

"That's it." Rachel stood quickly. "I knew I recognized that code."

She ran over to where her computer sat next to the large screen. Paige looked at Scott, who shrugged his shoulders.

Rachel pulled up another computer program and turned towards them. "See?" She looked at both of them expectantly.

Paige drew in a quick breath. "What program is this, Rachel?"

"One that my father and I wrote for our security system. There is a fail safe that will send a message along with specified files to this IP address should our firewalls be completely breached."

"Someone care to translate for me?" Scott asked.

"Rachel is saying that the part of this ghostcode" —she pointed to the one on her computer— "was written originally by your father."

Chapter 13

"D AD IS THE ONE trying to get your calculations?" Scott may not have the best relationship with the man, but he found it hard to believe that his dad would steal from Paige.

"Not necessarily." Paige tapped her fingers on the computer keys. "He could have taught this code to someone and then they used it."

"How do you know someone else didn't come up with the same code?" Tylan, who had been quiet through the whole exchange, spoke up. "Wouldn't all codes that give the same command look the same?"

Rachel tilted her head as if considering his question. "Answer me this. If you gave two different engineers the same materials to build a bridge, would the two bridges be the same?"

"I see your point," Tylan conceded. "So we can be sure that Charles either wrote this, or showed someone how he wrote it."

Rachel shifted her weight.

"Rachel, what is it?" Scott fixed his gaze on his sister

She pushed off her chair and paced. "Computer coding is one thing that Dad did teach me. We built the security measures of the bunker together."

"And?" Scott drew out the word.

Rachel winced. "I may have taught pieces of it to Mateo and his friend, Cole Donaldson."

"Does Dad know about this?"

"Of course. After all the secrets he kept from us, I vowed to never keep secrets from family," Rachel snapped.

Scott put his hands up in surrender. "I get it."

"It's an attempt at being smart." Paige shrugged one shoulder. "Using someone else's signature code points the finger at them. The problem is that there are only four people who know that code. It would have been smart to steal the code without their knowledge and use it."

Scott raised both of his eyebrows.

"That's assuming that one of the two guys is the writer of this code."

"It's a lead we can run down." Tylan nodded at her.

Paige looked away. "You don't need to help me. You are doing enough, helping find Heather."

"A friend of the Craftons is a friend of mine." The words were meant for Paige, but they wormed their way through him. Tylan was there for the fallout with his dad. He was the one that encouraged Scott to sign up for the Marines with him even though Scott ended up in the Air Force, that solidarity meant the world to him. How could Scott have neglected his friend for so long?

"Please let me pay for your help. You are a professional and it's only right."

Tylan gave her a lopsided grin. "You can pay the same rate as the Craftons."

Paige seemed satisfied with the answer. Scott thought he should set the record straight. He leaned in, putting his hand on the small of her back. She stiffened at first, but relaxed into his touch.

He whispered into her ear, "Pro bono."

She stiffened again and swung around to meet his eyes. She was gorgeous. He hoped the fire in her eyes never dimmed. The corners of his mouth rose slowly as he stared at her.

Her eyes searched his face looking for a truth to his words.

Tylan chuckled. "You two are good for each other."

"We're not..."

"No way, man..." they said in unison. Their response had Tylan shaking his head. Even though he said the words, his heart agreed with the man's assessment. They were good together.

"You might want to check this out." Tylan pointed to his screen. "Here are the death certificates that were filed by Heather's parents."

Tylan clicked over to a new window.

"Wait." Rachel took the computer and plugged it into one of the cords by the big monitors. "Now we can all see."

Tylan continued. "I've been looking through the files you gave me. Your dad has collected several newspaper articles from across the country. All about a pair of con artists posing as movers and then stealing paintings and replacing them with fakes. People didn't know that the exchange occurred until months or even years later. It's a brilliant scheme."

"So what does this have to do with Heather? Was she one of the con artists?" Scott held on to hope that the girl was not trafficked for sex, but somehow went straight to conning people.

"Only one of the articles gives a vague description of the two, but the woman shares a similar description as Heather," Tylan concluded.

"When was the most current article printed? Could we create a map and timeline to see where she was?" Scott was already trying to put together a mental picture of the last twelve years.

"Your father had the same idea." Tylan clicked on another open file and a map with markers indicating the dates of the crimes filled the screen. "It looks like the dates started about eight years ago and last year they stopped." Tylan studied the map.

"That doesn't mean she hasn't stopped. It just means it hasn't been reported yet," Rachel said.

"I don't think that Heather is doing this willingly."

All heads turned towards Scott.

"She told me that she did all she could and Dad had to figure out the rest."

Paige's eyes softened. "If she's a con artist, that could have easily been a lie."

It was the truth, but that didn't soften the blow. Scott winced. He would have to remember that Heather would not be the same sixteen-year-old girl she was when she was taken.

"Another question to ask," Tylan said hesitantly, " what happened those first four years?"

"I never wish anyone into a life of crime, but for her sake, I hope that she was only being trained to be a con artist." Paige's words mimicked his own sentiment.

"It looks like your dad was trying to figure out the criminal organization that she was caught up in." Tylan swiped the screen up to show a virtual evidence board.

In the center he had the words, "Who is Malinoe?" Following the lines and circles it looked like there were at least four other people working under the leader. Next to one name, Dolos, he had written Heather's name.

"Do we know who this Dolos is?"

"Well it all looks like Greek to me," Rachel said.

Scott gave her a curious look. "What looks like Greek? It's all in English." Had his sister lost it?

"No," she said with an exasperated sigh. "Each of these names is someone in Greek mythology. Dolos was the master of all con artists. Malinoe was a nymph known as the bringer of nightmares and mischief." She pointed to the other three names, "Pyroeis is the god of the wandering star, coming from the Greek word pyra meaning fire. Eros was the god of sexual attraction, doing the bidding of Aphrodite. Hermes was known as the messenger of the gods, but he is also the god of gambling."

There were no pictures next to any of the names, but there was something written under Hermes.

"Tylan, can you zoom in on Hermes?"

Tylan enlarged the area. Under the name there were lists of casinos, restaurants, and an online gambling site. Below all of that was the name Melton Fox.

Tylan gave a low growl. Melton was the reason his wife had died. To see the man's name in association with a possible criminal world would give any man cause for anger.

"I knew I never liked that man," Rachel grounded out.

"Dad never shared this with you?"

Rachel blinked a few times, "He still has his secrets apparently."

"If he knew that Melton was a bad egg, why didn't he say something when the man killed my wife?" Tylan's icy words hung in the air.

"The only way to know the answer to that question is to ask the man himself. Let's first look at the other names to learn as much as we can from his research before confronting him."

The conversation with his dad was sure to be an uncomfortable one, but he had enough of the man's secrets. Heather was still alive and Scott was going to do what he had to in order to reunite her with her family.

None of the other names had possible names assigned to them, but Eros had the words "sex trafficking" written underneath. Scott's stomach turned to granite. How could such evil find its way to the sleepy town of New Freedom?

He shared a look with Tylan before addressing the group.

"I'm going to the hospital to talk with Dad about everything he knows about Malinoe. Paige, you and Rachel stay here with Tylan. Continue to work through the files from

Dad's computer or if you need to keep looking through the computer code." Scott checked the time. "On second thought, we should all get some rest. It's late and the hospital won't let me in at this time of night. I'll go first thing in the morning."

"I'm going with you," Rachel said. A determined set to her jaw said she would fight him the whole way. "You can't keep me from visiting my own father."

"I want to go with you to ask him about the computer code. He might have insight that we're not thinking about." Paige stood with her hands on her hips.

Why did he surround himself with such head strong women?

He looked at Tylan for some backup, but the man wisely chose to stay out of it, raising his hands in surrender.

He sighed. "Fine, but don't go off on your own. You should have someone with you at all times."

Rachel rolled her eyes, "Okay, Griz. Sometimes your love is annoying."

"Just trying to keep you both alive. I'm on duty tomorrow, so we'll have to swing by the station so I can check in and get the chief's truck."

"I'm on duty tomorrow too, but I'll register as off-site and pick up my gear," Tylan added.

The new tele-notification system gave volunteers the option to check-in at the station and take their gear with them. This allowed people to show up at school, family gatherings, or other events with the knowledge that they couldn't be further than twenty minutes from the station, which was almost in the middle of town. If an alert went out, it was expected for the volunteer to accept the call on their device and get to the site as soon as possible in full gear.

"It's a plan, then. We'll meet you at the station at 0700." Scott nodded.

As they all climbed the stairs, Paige tried to hide a yawn behind her hand.

"I should get back to my camper to get some rest."

"You aren't going to be out there alone." Scott stepped in front of her once he topped the stairs.

She quirked an eyebrow at him. "I have been on my own for the last four years. I think I can handle one more night."

"That may be so, but I would breathe better knowing that you were in a space with walls anchored into the ground."

"I never had a sleepover as a kid," Rachel piped in. "We could fulfill a childhood desire of mine if you slept over in my room tonight."

The fight went out of her. "Fine. Let me go get my stuff. I used my extra set of clothes from my jump bag." She faced Scott. "Do you mind taking me to my camper?"

"Lead the way, Doc." Scott sent Rachel a look of gratitude. She smiled in return.

At 0500, Scott rose from a fitful night's sleep. Between the threats against Paige, seeing Heather Zeits in the flesh, and his father's evidence board, Scott spun theories and ideas around in his head most of the night.

A run would help him clear the fog in his head. He laced up his shoes and grabbed his weighted pack. During wildland fire fighting training, he would run miles in full gear. The weighted pack was an easy substitute and helped him stay in shape to carry all of the gear he needed in an emergency. The last thing the company needed was a fireman that literally couldn't pull their own weight.

Crisp spring morning air made his lungs burn slightly, but the burn kept him pushing harder. It had been a few days since it rained and the trails were no longer slick with mud. The run is exactly what he needed. Scott topped the mountain and took in the view. Below him in the valley to the north was New Freedom. It had grown in size over the last twelve years, but it still had the same small town charm he grew to love as a child.

Scott turned to the south and the state forest abutting his parent's property stretching for acres. At one point in history, the land had been almost destroyed by lumber companies seeking its large oak, chestnut, and elm trees. Over the years, the state bought the land and restored the forest. It allowed logging to occur, but it was restricted to certain areas and was monitored heavily.

He took note of the overall health of the forest. This was his home. No matter how far he traveled with the Air Force, these forested lands were always going to be home.

He closed his eyes. "Lord, I know that You are at work here, but I could use a bit of guidance." Scott waited for a small voice or a verse to be put on his heart. Only soul settling peace filled him. Not the answer he was hoping for, but he would take it.

Running down hill was harder on his aging knees, but despite the pain his return run was faster than the uphill climb. As he stomped up the steps after doing some cooling stretches, the door to the cabin flew open. Paige slammed right into his chest.

He put his hands on her arms. "Where's the fire, Doc?"

Paige pushed off of his chest and glared at him. "There you are. Rachel told me not to worry, but we didn't know where you were."

She was worried about him. A slow grin curved his lips. "Thanks for coming to find me."

Paige opened her mouth slightly. Those sweet pinked lips called to him. What would it be like to claim them? To give in to the desires stirring inside him? Before he could cave and claim something he had no right to, Scott stepped to the side of her.

"I need to shower, then we can grab some food and get to the station."

She said nothing in return. He looked back at her expecting relief to show on her face, but she looked almost hurt like his brush-off had disappointed her.

The ride to the station was short and done in relative silence. He liked that about Paige. She didn't need to fill the void with idle chatter.

Rachel drove their father's old truck in front of them. She didn't want to be stranded at the hospital if he was called in. He was thankful for the time alone with Paige.

"I've been trying to figure out how your abduction and Agent Rollands' murder fit in with all that we have discovered." Scott voiced his inner dialog.

"I'm not convinced that it is. Although if this Malinoe character is into human trafficking, I could see how he would be threatened by my program."

Scott sat up a bit straighter. "Can you unpack that for me?"

"I was going to wait until we were at the hospital, but I got clearance to tell you about Project Searchlight."

"I like the name. What is it exactly?"

"In conjunction with engineers developing cameras to complement my work, I was tasked with developing a facial recognition program. Unlike current programs, the one that I developed takes measurements to the micrometer giving us a higher rate of confirmation at quicker speeds. The new cameras will allow us to scan for blood vessel heat signatures as well."

"I'm not sure how they got the heat signature technology to work on such a finite level, but that's amazing. Why blood vessels?"

"When people alter their appearance, the silicone rubber used looks like skin and has a similar density as skin. This has been an issue with current facial recognition software that base their scans on density, but the face like the rest of your skin has blood vessels in the epidermis. Using the new camera technology allows us to scan the face underneath the silicone giving us a true facial scan."

"Impressive." Scott had new respect for the woman. She was truly brilliant. But there was something more behind it, he could sense it. This research was personal to her.

"How did you come up with the idea?"

Paige stared out the windshield, he wasn't sure she would answer him.

"I told you how Hank died, but there is more to that story." She played with the hem of her shirt. "The man responsible for using the RPG had used a facial prosthetic to look like one of the soldiers on base. When they reviewed the video surveillance they were able to identify the soldier. A manhunt ensued and the body of the soldier was found." She dropped her head. Her next words were so soft that Scott strained to hear her. "The problem was he had been dead before the RPG was fired."

She fell silent gathering her thoughts. "They never found out who killed them. The facial recognition programs only pinged the dead soldier and there was no other trace evidence left behind."

"It was strange that the insurgent would have hidden his identity like that," Scott wondered out loud.

"I thought so too. It's why, when I met the engineer developing the camera technology for the medical field, I knew that I needed to create the facial recognition program to complement it. I didn't want the lack of justice that happened to Hank to happen to someone else."

Scott reached over. "We will figure this out. The good news is that your program won't do as much good without the new camera tech."

She whipped her head towards him. "I hadn't considered that. Agent Hunter said that a prototype of the camera was stolen two weeks ago. It was an early version, but in the right hands it could prove to be a problem."

This just turned more dangerous. The only thing standing between someone selling the completed technology on the dark web was Paige. They needed answers from his father. He wasn't going to let anything happen to Paige.

Chapter 14

S COTT FOUND A SPOT to park in the visitor parking lot. There was a short walk to the front doors, but it was daylight and there were few cars in the lots this early, so he could see anyone approaching. Paige fidgeted in her seat. Scott knew she wanted to say something, but he waited until she was ready.

"This is going to sound awkward, but with everything that is happening I can't shake this feeling that one of us might need it."

Scott rode out the lull.

"Can I have your number?" Paige bit her lower lip and looked at him with expectancy.

A slow grin filled his face. "Is that all you want?"

Paige stared at him in shock because of his forward answer. It seemed like his heart kept winning out over his head, and for the first time he didn't want to shove her away. He took her phone from her slacked grip and sent himself a text message.

"There. Now, we have each other's numbers." He winked and circled the truck as quickly as he could to open her door for her.

By the time he made it to her door, she had snapped out of her stupor.

"Thanks," she said as she made a quick line for the hospital. She was moving faster than a fireman racing towards an unmanned nozzle. He would have to cool it, if he didn't want to scare her away. She had lost everyone that she had ever loved. Those were hurts that cut deep, but he could be patient.

Rachel was standing outside their mother's door. Her eyes were darting around and she shifted her weight from foot to foot. What made her nervous?

"Rachel, what's going on?" Scott asked as he approached.

"Mom is being discharged, but she is refusing to go home because Dad is still here."

"Wait. Back up. They are discharging Mom? They don't discharge patients from the ICU." Scott turned to see if he could find a nurse or doctor that could explain what was going on.

"She should have been taken out of the ICU yesterday, but apparently Mom can be persuasive and they agreed to let her stay in her room until they needed the bed for a patient that actually needed the care in the ICU."

Scott's shoulders relaxed a bit. "Mom does tend to get her way when she wants to use her skills. Is she in her room?"

Rachel shook her head. "She wanted a moment with Dad before you got here. I think she may be giving him a piece of her mind for not telling you anything."

Scot gave a soft chuckle. "Then we better go save Dad."

Scott grabbed Paige's hand on reflex. When his brain caught up to his heart, he waited with anticipation to see her reaction. He wouldn't let go of her hand unless she was the one that released his. To his surprise, she slid her slender fingers around his large hand and tightened her grip. Whatever battle she was fighting in the parking lot was either over or she was choosing to enjoy the moment. Whichever reason, Scott would relish the feel of her hand in his.

Scott pushed back the curtain inside the door of his dad's room. His mom sat in the recliner, reading one of her books as Dad was sitting in the bed scribbling on a piece of paper.

Without looking up from the paper, Dad greeted him. "I was hoping you would be by today."

Finished for the moment with what he was writing, he raised his head to meet Scott's gaze. Charles looked more like himself. The color had started to return to his parlor. Scott wanted to sigh in relief, but he didn't want his father to know how much he was worried about his health.

"You look better," Scott said with a slight shrug of one shoulder.

"God was watching over me." His eyes flicked down for a moment to take in Scott's and Paige's hands. "I see you've met Paige."

Paola stood. "Paige, you take my seat. I'm going to see if I can chase down that doctor who promised to sign my discharge papers." The door clicked shut quietly.

Paige let go of his hand and he missed the grounded feeling it gave him. She sat in his mother's vacated seat, looking at him to lead the conversation.

Scott had rehearsed on the way to the hospital how he would approach the subject, but none of the options seemed like the right way to start.

"I saw Heather yesterday," he blurted before his brain made up its mind how to proceed.

His dad sat up straighter in the bed. "Is she alright? Were you able to persuade her to come back?"

Scott shook his head. "She looked mad. Said that she did what she could and you had to figure it out." Scott rested his hands on the end of the hospital bed. "What is going on, Dad?"

He kept the evidence board information locked away. He wanted to see what his father revealed first.

"When I got back from my last assignment and discovered you had left," Dad leaned back in his bed, "your mother persuaded me to reconsider what you said."

Scott could only imagine how that conversation had gone. His mother was probably the only person that could change the man's mind.

Charles blew out a breath. "I retired from the company, mostly, and spent the first two years calling in favors to track down Heather. Every time I got close they moved her. I wasn't sure how they knew I was getting close or if it was just dumb luck."

He sat up straight and stared at Scott. "When Mark and Shirley declared her dead seven years ago and had a funeral, they told me to move on, but I couldn't let it go. I officially started my new organization, Kora, to help families find their loved ones. Especially working with those who couldn't afford PIs or other security agencies to do the work for them. We've been able to help numerous families be reunited. Some of the people that we rescue find themselves in danger of being discovered, so we've had to develop a type of witness protection program. We've been expanding the organization and have several people in town on the roll. Most are volunteers."

"One day you'll have to tell me who all is involved and the significance behind the name."

Charles nodded, then leaned his head back against his pillow as if gathering strength to finish the story. "Six years ago, a contact in the realm of high art said that he thought he may have seen Heather."

"A year after you stopped looking for her?"

"I never stopped looking for her," Dad snapped, then closed his eyes. "Every time a lead would come up, I would drop everything to trace it down, but never to any solid end." He scrubbed his face and stared at Scott with sadness tinging his eyes. "My contact, let's call him Eddy, he has a photographic memory. He never forgets anything he sees. Heather appeared on the arm of some well-to-do millionaire at the opening of an art show in Manhattan. I started to trace her and noticed a pattern of stolen art. It took me close to four years before I finally caught up to her."

"Wait. You found her and you didn't bring her home?" Anger boiled in Scott's stomach.

His dad pinned him with a look that dared him to say that again. "You saw her. Even spoke with her and she still ran away. Back to them."

"Fair point. So what happened?"

"She convinced me to leave her there. She was trying to take down the people who stole her life. I told her to memorize my personal number and call me using a new burner phone with leads I could run down for her. This kept her safer while she still stayed on the inside. I also agreed to not tell her parents until she was clear from the organization. She may have to go into witness protection and it would be safer for them to think she is dead than be in danger with the knowledge that she was still alive."

Scott didn't necessarily agree with that logic, but he'd let it slide for now.

"That explains the evidence board," he murmured.

"I see you found our work. We figured out who Hermes was, but then he killed Fahta and himself before I could confront him."

"Why didn't you tell the police about your suspicions when Melton died?"

Charles sighed and Scott could feel the weight that his father carried. "Since Melton was the fire chief, I didn't know who else was on the payroll. There could be cops or other higher ranking officials. Fox was into gambling and manipulation. People will do crazy things to keep their secrets safe. I think that whoever runs the organization forced Fox to kill Fahta."

"Have you told Tylan?" This from Paige.

Charles looked at her. "I was going to, but wanted to run down my newest lead, which landed me here."

Scott needed to refocus the conversation. "How does Heather fit into this organization?"

"When they discovered her hacking skills, she was assigned to help Dolos. He is the man who controls which pieces of art are to be stolen. She has never seen the man's face and has been trying to figure out his true identity."

The paintings found at the Zeits house now made sense. He hoped that the FBI was able to figure out where they went.

"Malinoe is the leader," Scott filled in, and his dad nodded. "What about the other two?"

"She hasn't had much interaction with them, so information is limited. Pyroeis is the one that gets them secure places to store stolen items before they are sold. She doesn't interact with him more than a text with an address. But she's fairly certain he sets the place on fire when they move on to get rid of all the evidence."

Could he be the arsonist they were looking for in the area?

That only left Eros. Scott tried to swallow the bile rising in his throat. Human trafficking was an evil all too prevalent in the world.

"What about Eros? Does she know anything about him?"

His father looked at Paige, then back to Scott. "He is the one who procures people. Whether that's people to steal art from, target for blackmail, suck into gambling debts, or even sell. Eros is the one who finds people to exploit." His father's tone grew very dark. "A few days ago, Heather sent me an encrypted message." His eyes turned hard. "Eros is after Paige."

"Me?" Paige squeaked out.

Charles nodded grimly. "When Mateo came to me about what he overheard, I was scared that Heather had slipped up. I was trying to track her down when we were run off the road."

Paige looked dazed. "The threat would explain the abduction attempt and Agent Rollands' death."

"Rollands is dead?" Dad asked.

"They are not sure of the cause of death, but he left me a note before he died warning me of a ghostcode in my program."

Charles gave her his full attention. "Did you find the code he warned you about?"

Paige looked at Scott, then back to Dad. "Rachel and I combed through the program and found a ghostcode embedded that took a snapshot of the other ghostcode calculations and sent them to an unfamiliar IP address."

"Please tell me you were able to remove it."

"Rachel took care of that for me last night." Paige played with the hem of her shirt. Scott was beginning to recognize that as a nervous habit. "Rachel recognized the send code as one you taught to her for your security system. She showed it to two others."

"We are following up with those two leads," Scott interjected. "Dad, we need to know, did you teach anyone else that specific line of code? Or know of any security breaches to your system?"

"Rachel monitors the system for us and she is the only one that I taught that code."

Could Rachel be the one who planted that ghostcode? No. She was the one that pointed it out last night, and Paige watched her remove it from the program. She double checked her work.

"What I don't get is when would anyone have the opportunity to insert the code into the program?" she thought aloud.

"Did you ever leave your computer unattended or not locked away?" Charles asked.

"I always have it with me or locked in my trailer while I'm at the station."

"What about the rest of your computer? Did you check for a point of entry breach on the computer itself?" Charles' words were coming slower. "Also check the cameras around your trailer. We might catch the hacker on tape."

She was thankful to have come here today, but they needed to let the man rest.

Reaching out, she squeezed his hand. "Thanks for helping us. We'll look into those things and let you know what we find."

Charles gripped her hand firmly. "Stay safe, Paige. These people are dangerous. If they take you, stay alive." He looked at Scott briefly before pinning her with his gaze. "We will find you."

He released her hand and sent a hard look at his son. "Don't let her out of your sight."

"Wasn't planning on it." The protective stare of his eyes made her breath catch. She wasn't alone anymore and she didn't think she ever wanted to be there again.

Paige rose from the chair making her way towards the door. Scott waited for her to pass, placing his hand on the small of her back. The touch gave her strength, because if she were honest with herself, Charles' ominous warning had her worried.

Stepping into the hall, Paige spotted Rachel and Paola waiting for them at the nurses station.

"Mom wants to go home to shower before returning to be with Dad." Rachel stepped forward and searched her face as if looking for something.

"What's wrong?" Paige asked cautiously.

"Mom just told me about Eros' message. I just wanted to make sure how you were doing knowing a whole criminal organization was after you."

"Well, when you put it that way, I'm living my best life," Paige deadpanned.

Rachel tilted her head and pulled her eyebrows together.

Paige resisted the urge to roll her eyes. "I'm terrified. Some powerful evil is after me and the federal agent assigned to keep me safe was killed." She took a deep breath and turned her head to see Scott's face. "I'm not alone and that gives me courage to keep going."

Scott slid his hand into hers and interlocked their fingers. The movement was smooth as if they had done it a thousand times before. Paola's face beamed as she watched them interact, and Rachel gave her a wink.

"It's about time." Rachel folded her arms across her chest with a smirk on her face.

"Are you ready to go, Mrs. Crafton?" Paige asked, changing the subject.

"Paige, you know you are to call me Paola, and yes. I got the paperwork right here." She held up the small stack of papers.

"Let's get you home and feeling more normal," Rachel said.

They took the elevator down to the front lobby through the cafe. Scott stopped at a table near the front panel of windows. "Why don't you and Mom stay inside while Rachel and I go get the vehicles?"

"We can walk out with you," Paola protested.

"The parking lot is filling up with cars quickly and I don't like not being able to see far. It would leave Paige too exposed."

Understanding dawned on Paola's face. "Go. We will be safe inside the hospital."

He turned to Paige. "Please stay inside until we pull up with the trucks."

Before she could talk herself out of it, Paige stood on her toes and kissed his smooth cheek. "I promise."

The smoldering desire in his eyes made her heart race, but when he smiled she had to fight to stay on her feet. She could get used to this kind of intoxication.

Rachel cleared her throat. Scott stepped back into full on protector mode. She hoped there were more of those moments in their future.

She watched Rachel and Scott jog out the door and into the rows of cars.

"Shoot." Paola looked through her bag. "I forgot my cell phone upstairs in Charles' room."

She turned to go back to the elevators. Paige didn't want her to overdo it. It had only been a few days since she received a concussion.

"Wait here. I'll run up and get it for you."

Paola started to shake her head, but stopped. "I'm supposed to be looking out for you."

"You said it yourself, I'll be safe inside the hospital."

Paola was rubbing her head, probably trying to get the pain to go away. She blew out a breath. "It is on the bedside table closest to the door."

Paige took off towards the elevators. She wanted to be back before Scott and Rachel pulled up to the doors.

She felt, rather than saw, someone step in behind her.

"We can do this the easy way, or you can resist and I blow up the Chief's truck."

Paige stiffened. "What do you want?"

179

The man spoke in a low whisper so no one around them could hear. "We are going on a little walk." He shoved her toward the stairs. "Down."

They descended the stairs in silence. Besides a few offices and a laundry facility the only other thing in the basement was the morgue. Paige swallowed. Where could he be taking her?

They wove through the hallway towards a loading dock. A door that read, *Employees Only* was to the right of the rolling dock door. They headed out that door. Paige saw a parking lot ahead of them. He parked in the employee lot. It was nowhere near shift change so there was no one around that she could see.

He was smart. Something about his voice seemed familiar too. Although he was trying to disguise it, the sound tried to pull at a memory in her brain.

"White laundry van straight back." He gave the gruff order with a shove.

Paige stumbled forward but caught herself. She finally got to look at the man's face, but he wore a cap, sunglasses, and a sweater with its hood up. She couldn't make out any of his facial features.

"Turn forward and walk."

If she screamed, would anyone be close enough to hear her? *If they take you, stay alive.* Charles' words echoed in her brain. She could do that.

If only she knew how the guy intended to blow up Scott's truck. She could fight her way out, but if he hit a detonator or sent a text before she could stop him, then Scott would be injured, or worse, dead.

Images of the fireball that engulfed the helio with Hank inside filled her brain. She couldn't lose another man to an explosion. Not if she could keep him alive.

We will find you. Peace washed through Paige.

Scott would find her. Until then she needed to gather as much information from her captor as possible.

Chapter 15

"**W**HAT DO YOU WANT from me?" Paige asked as the man shoved her forward.

A deep throated grunt came from the man, "You will see."

"Does this have anything to do with the ghostcode?" She had to try and get him to talk.

"For a soldier, you are having a hard time following orders." He spoke through gritted teeth.

She needed to be careful. She didn't want him to blow up Scott's truck out of spite even though she was still walking towards the van willingly.

God had answered her prayers about saving Charles—maybe He might spare her life too. *God, if you're listening, I could use a little help.*

As they drew closer to the van, every survival instinct she had was screaming to not get into the van.

She was running through possible moves in her head. Calculating the distance to the van, the space between vehicles, and the chances of the man taking her being trained in hand to hand combat.

The bomb. She needed a way to make sure he didn't set off that bomb.

Paige stopped and swung to face her captor.

"What are you doing? I will blow up lover boy's truck."

"I will continue to go with you willingly, but you need to let me text them. Otherwise they'll never stop hunting you, Eros."

It was a risk using his code name, but she figured it was worth the guess.

The man slowly clapped. No detonator in his hands, but that's not to say it wasn't in his sweater pocket. Or it could be wired with a cell phone and one call or text would set it off.

"Congratulations for figuring that part out. Too bad someone else wants you. You would have been fun to break."

The menace in his words sent a chill down her back. Who was this man? Charles said that he was the one who found people to exploit. She said another prayer that the exploitation of her was only for her research or intelligence and not her body.

She swallowed. "Who wants me?"

"Enough questions." Eros grabbed her arm and spun her around.

They were only one row from the van. Movement in the wooded area caught her eye. Could that be Scott? Or someone else here to help her?

She kept her eye on the van in hopes of not drawing attention to the hopeful rescue on its way.

"You know that I work for the Department of Defense." She spoke over her shoulder. "If you let me go now, I won't report this. Taking me will only bring the full force of the government down on you."

The man gave a disgusted grunt. "The government has been trying to find me for almost a decade."

He grabbed her arm and reached around her for the door. It was now or never. Paige used the momentary distraction to swing her hand out and connect with his windpipe. The man loosened his grip on her arm, which allowed her to tear free. The tight space between the vehicles prevented her from being able to kick out, so she settled for using her knee to find the softest spot on the male body.

As he was gasping for air and bent over in pain, Paige took off running as fast as she could from the man trying to capture her. She looked over her shoulder to see if he was chasing her when she ran into a solid wall. The spicy aftershave enveloped her and she relaxed into Scott's arms. She knew she needed to get herself together, but the tears wouldn't stop this time.

"Shh. You're okay. I've got you." He rubbed her back gently. The soothing words and motion calmed her down quickly.

She pulled away. "If we hurry, we can probably chase him down."

The sound of squealing tires made her spin around. The white van was pulling out of the back parking lot ignoring the red light. Thankfully, no one crashed into them, preventing more injuries today.

Tylan came running up, barely winded from his sprint across the parking lot.

"Sorry, I tried to get to him after Paige disabled him, but he jumped in the van and took off." He gave a half grin to Paige. "Nice moves, by the way. You should have seen her, Griz. We might have to call her Griz too. Or maybe Grizzie."

She appreciated Tylan's ability to lighten the mood. "Someone will have to tell me the story behind that name."

Scott gave her a boyish grin. "I look forward to that day, but for now we should get you out of here and somewhere safe."

"You both are on duty. We can go to the station," Paige offered. "There are cameras there where we can watch all the entrances and I can lock myself in the women's bunkroom if I have to. Besides, you need to work on that report for the mayor and I need to finish running my diagnostic on the program and check my computer for a breach."

"We could set up shop in the conference room," Tylan suggested.

Scott gave him a look that asked for an explanation.

"I wanted to go through your father's files again to see if I couldn't run down more leads. Especially against Eros since he is an active threat against Paige right now. We can work the others later, but the more information we know about our opponent the better our chances of stopping them."

"The conference room can be locked." Paige was liking this plan more. "It would allow me to work on the program with more security. I'd be working offline anyway."

Scott took her hand and started walking towards the front of the hospital. "Tylan, I'd like for you to comb through the video footage around Paige's trailer. Maybe we can catch this guy sneaking into her place."

"On it. I'm going to stop at the bunker and get my computer. I'll meet you at the station." Tylan jogged away.

As Paige watched his retreating figure, she asked, "How did he get here so fast?"

"I texted him as soon as Dad told me about the active threat against you. He served as a Marine guard at US embassies across the world. He's one you want watching out for you and I wanted only the best looking out for the...for you."

What was he going to say? She knew that they shared feelings for each other. How serious were his feelings? For now, she needed to focus on getting the program to DC and staying out of the hands of Eros.

The front of the hospital came into view and she saw Rachel standing guard by both trucks. Adrenaline started pumping through Paige's veins again. The bomb.

She took off running, still holding Scott's hand, "The man who took me said if I didn't come with him quietly, he would blow up your truck."

Scott ran past her, covering the distance to the truck in a few brief seconds. He fell to his knees and crawled under the truck. Rachel's confusion evaporated when she saw him crawl underneath. Before Paige could tell her any-thing, Rachel flew to the other side and slid under.

"What are you...never mind. Help me look for wires or explosives."

The two siblings were under the vehicle for what felt like hours, but really was only a few minutes. Scott and Rachel made their way to standing and came to where Paige had stopped running.

"There is no bomb." Scott brushed the dirt from his pants.

Paige felt her knees wobble a bit. "I went with him because I didn't want anything to happen to you. When I saw movement in the tree line, I thought it was you." The words were spilling from her. "Since you were safe, I decided to make a run for it."

Scott wrapped his strong arms around. "Everyone is safe. You did a great job."

He held her against his chest and rested his cheek on the top of her head. She wanted to stay here, but knew they needed to figure out who Eros was and take him down. If they got lucky enough, they'd take the whole organization with him.

Reluctantly, she pulled back. "Thanks."

Joy danced in his eyes. "Anytime."

Paige took another step away. "We should get back to the station."

"I'll take Mom home to freshen up, and then we'll come back here to be with Dad." Distracted by the closeness of Scott, Paige had forgotten that Rachel was standing nearby. She faced her friend who was beaming at them.

"Keep us posted on your progress?" Scott actually asked this time instead of commanded.

Rachel straightened her shoulders and stood tall. "I'll keep them safe. You, Paige, and Tylan go figure out who is doing this."

"Thanks, Rach." A moment of mutual respect passed between them.

Rachel moved to the older truck parked behind them where their mother sat in the passenger seat. Paige made eye contact with her and the woman had transformed from loving, kind mother of her friend to a fierce warrior. Paige was surrounded by people who would protect her, even to their own demise. The thought both gave her comfort and made her fearful. These were good people, she didn't want any of them to be injured or worse because of her.

Scott stepped close and lowered his voice. "Don't go there. You were willing to sacrifice yourself to keep me safe. Please don't pull away from me. I don't think my heart could handle it."

His whispered confession had her own heart racing. Whatever was happening between the two of them, he felt it too. She didn't respond with words, but took his hand. They would figure this out together.

By the time they made it to the fire station Tylan was already there with his computer. He had turned the meeting in progress sign around so that everyone knew the room was occupied.

Tylan took a rectangle object from his bag and slid it over the top of his laptop. Opening two flaps, he now had two more monitors framing his main screen.

"I may be the one with screen envy now," Paige confessed.

Tylan barked a laugh. "Proper research requires multiple screens. I had Ronnie bring me the extensions from our office."

"Nice."

"I'm going to check in with Tucker. I'll be in my office if you need me," Scott said from the door.

Tylan and Scott shared a look.

"I'll be fine. Go do your work and I'll do mine." Paige shooed him down the hall.

Taking a seat at the opposite end of the table from Tylan, she brought up a diagnostic scanner first. Checking her computer for a breach was the first thing she needed to do. With the scan running, she double checked that her computer was in a bubble before opening her program.

Tylan and Paige fell into a comfortable silence as they both worked their separate problems. She needed to go through the last set of calculations to make sure the algorithm was working properly. He was looking for any clues for the identity of Eros.

Tylan gave a soft grunt. Paige snapped her eyes to him. "What did you find?"

"Charles was able to trace Eros last known location to Indiana, Pennsylvania. He credits him with the disappearance of three young women. That was over a year ago. Before that, he has him in Bryson City, North Carolina and four other small towns along the East Coast."

"Smaller towns have less resources and wouldn't necessarily be able to connect the crimes like Charles has."

"True, but it would be hard to disappear in a small town where everyone knows everyone else." Tylan paused to type something, "Brilliant."

"Don't go having respect for a man who preys on women and sells them for who-knows-what purpose."

Tylan's face hardened and he clenched the hand sitting on the table into a fist. "I would never have respect for someone like that." He gritted through his teeth. "The man targets smaller towns, but not too small so that he is unable to blend in. He probably has some kind of job that helps to deflect any suspicion away from himself."

"Or he helps the community on a volunteer basis." Paige added. "That doesn't narrow down the pool here in New Freedom."

Tylan stared at the wall for a moment. "When did you arrive in New Freedom?"

"Eight months ago. I see where you're headed. So we are looking for someone who moved here after I did, and who does something good for the town whether through their job or volunteer work."

"I'll start working on a list of people that moved here after you arrived. It won't be a comprehensive list by any stretch, but it'll be a start. I'll ask Ronnie to make one too."

Paige felt better now that they had a lead, even if the lead was a long shot. It was something to look into.

Before she could resume her perusal of the final calculations, her phone rang. Hunter.

"I've got to take this."

"I'll step out into the hallway." Tylan grabbed the notepad he was working with and closed the door behind him.

Paige answered. "Agent Hunter, do you have news for me about Rollands?"

"DCIS Agent Wilson should be making contact with you today about that. I will let him fill in the details as he sees fit." Translation, no one would tell her anything useful. "I'm calling about the program. Were you able to complete it? I have the Secretary of Defense breathing down my neck to secure the program ever since the camera prototype was stolen."

Paige breathed through her nose. *Keep the sarcasm in check. He is a senior officer.* She repeated the reminder many times during basic and through her military career.

"I should be able to finish the calculations by the end of the day. I'll download the program on an external drive and give it to Agent Wilson. I don't want to expose it to a computer connected to the web until it is in a secure facility."

Hunter's harsh breath crackled across the line. "Fine. But put it in a locked case and send only me the combination."

"Do you not trust Wilson?"

"Wilson is as clean as they come. But if something happens to him, I want the drive to be as secure as possible."

She didn't want to argue that a locked case wouldn't keep the most skilled people away from the drive, but she kept her mouth shut. She would have the original if something would happen to the copy.

"Understood, sir."

"MacFarland."

"Yes, sir?"

"Be safe."

"Will do, sir." Apparently there is a heart in the statue that was Agent Hunter. Or he could just be trying to cover his own hide.

Paige walked to the door and let Tylan back in.

"What did DC want?"

"They wanted their program yesterday. I'm to give a secured hard drive to the DCIS agent here investigating Rollands murder."

"Seems about right." Tylan slid back into his chair.

"Guess I should finish my calculations and—" A ding from her computer drew her attention.

"What is it?" Tylan stayed on his side of the table, but gave her his full attention.

"I ran a diagnostic scan looking for when the computer was accessed." She scrolled through the log of the last two weeks. "There. Last Tuesday my computer was accessed while I was on shift. Whoever did this must have serious hacking skills, because logging into my computer is no easy task."

Tylan smirked. "Do I detect respect in your voice?"

Paige couldn't resist the eye roll. "No, just stating how protected I like to keep my tech. But given enough time and the right kind of skills, no computer is unhackable."

Tylan lifted one eyebrow. "Really?"

"Yes." Paige has seen and worked with some of the best hackers in the world. Thankfully they were on her side, or at least she thought they were.

"Can you pull up the cameras from my trailer and check last Tuesday's feed?"

"Give me a second." Tylan's fingers flew across the keys. "Bingo."

Paige came to stand behind him as he sped back through Tuesday's video.

"There." Paige pointed to a figure in dark clothes. There was a ball cap pulled low over his eyes and a backpack on his one shoulder. They watched as he easily picked the lock of the door and slipped inside. Eight hours later, according to the time stamp, he slipped out the door and took the time to lock it again, erasing any proof of the break in.

"Well, at least I know it took him a while to break through the firewalls. Not like that's any consolation to the fact that I got hacked." Paige blew out a breath. "I never should have left it at the camper unattended. We didn't even get a picture of his face. It's as if he knew the cameras were there."

"That's exactly what happened. It was no mistake that he avoided having his picture captured. We already know that we are dealing with an organization of criminals. This guy was either contracted out or is a soldier with a particular set of skills that they use when they need it. The question becomes, is the hack on your computer and the bounty on your head related? Or are you so lucky as to have two sets of criminals after you?"

"I hope they are connected. Otherwise, I've got a bigger problem." Paige returned to her computer. "Time to get this program back to DC where it can be safe. Then someone will have to pray that the attempts on my life will stop."

Tylan's head snapped up at her last comment. "My wife used to tell me that the Lord hears all the cries for help. Even the unspoken ones. And that His ways are the best despite what we think we want."

"Well, sometimes His ways don't feel like the best," Paige muttered.

Tylan's eyes darkened. "I know."

Paige knew that Fahta was killed in a car accident by Melton Fox, but didn't know her on a personal level. Maybe if Paige would have gone to church with Rachel when she asked her to do so, they would have met there.

Now that Melton Fox was implicated in criminal activity, Tylan had to be wondering about what actually caused the car crash. Paige remembered all too well the pain of losing the person you loved.

"Your wife sounds like a wonderful woman. I wish I would have known her better."

Paige finished running her final diagnostic and put a copy on a hard drive. The alarm in the station went off before Tylan could respond. Scott burst through the door.

"There's been an explosion at my parents' house."

Paige texted Rachel to secure the case from Scott's office at the station and only give it to Agent Wilson.

"I'm going with you." She pocketed her phone, not giving him a chance to respond.

Chapter 16

S COTT WAS TORN. HE needed to keep Paige safe, but his family and the company needed him to be fully engaged. He was trying to formulate a plan to do it all when Paige broke through his thought process.

"Go get your gear. I will meet you at your truck in one minute. I need to lock the external drive in the case."

With the beginnings of a plan in place, Scott ran for his locker inside the truck bay. After putting on turnout gear hundreds of times, he could do it in his sleep. By the time he was done putting on the gear and jogged over to the chief's truck, Paige was running out with her computer bag in hand.

She threw it in the back of the cab and jumped into the passenger seat. This situation couldn't get any worse. Not only was she leaving the security of the fire station, but he wouldn't be able to focus solely on her safety. Pile on top of that the fact his childhood home just exploded, and he couldn't imagine how this could get much worse.

"I promise to stay in the truck with the doors locked. I don't want to leave my computer unattended more than I have to."

Relief washed through him. "That sounds like the safest option right now. If for whatever reason you need to leave the truck, please tell me. I need to know that you're safe so I can focus on keeping everyone else safe."

She reached across the console where he had his computer and other gear to squeeze his arm. "I promise. Focus on getting that fire out and keeping our guys safe."

Now that they were on the same page as far as her safety was concerned, he wanted to bring up the report that was on his desk when they arrived at the station.

"I got preliminary findings on the Zeits fire," Scott began.

"Was it the same as the Miller and other fires? The ones accredited to the arsonist?"

"No. The Zeits fire was started by lighting the curtains in the upstairs bedroom on fire. This would allow whoever set it to escape out the back door before it caught too much else. It was also why we were able to save most of the house. Then there were the paintings found in the kitchen. The opposite side of the house where the blaze was set."

"So either the arsonist changed their MO, which is highly unlikely, or someone else set the Zeits fire. Maybe someone who wanted to get a message to the authorities without actually talking with them."

Scott had had the same thought. "What message is Heather sending us?"

"We don't know Heather set that fire."

"For the sake of argument, let's assume she did. Those paintings she left behind must have some kind of significance. But what?"

The question was left unanswered by either of them because the Craftons' house, completely engulfed in flames, came into view.

Scott pulled behind the second engine. Pulling his gear from the back, he headed towards the fire. Hampton had been the first on scene and was the field command. With one last glance at the truck to make sure Paige was still safe inside, Scott set off to find the FC.

"Hampton, what do we have?"

"The gas has been shut off to the street, the building is clear of all inhabitants. We have Team Alpha on the Charlie Delta side of the structure preventing the adjacent house from catching embers."

As if on cue a gust of wind blew through having the flames licking towards the tree line between the two houses. His parents lived at the end of the street, so only one neighboring house was close enough to worry about right now, but if the wind shifted, their efforts would have to change as well.

"You said there were no inhabitants inside."

"Yes, sir." Hampton softened his features. "Rachel met us here. She was the one who called it in." He nodded to a place behind Scott. Turning around, he saw both his mother and sister standing guard at his truck. Relief washed through him. His sister's face was stoic as she watched the fire consume their house. The only thing that gave away the severity of the situation was the single tear that traced down his mother's cheek.

Hot anger boiled in his gut. These people were going down, but for now he needed to focus on getting this fire out.

"I'm sending you and Gosnell over to alpha team. We need to contain the blaze."

Scott got on the radio and gave orders to each team. He would not risk the lives of his men when the chances of any part of the structure being salvageable were slim at best. With no civilians inside, they would focus their efforts on containing and extinguishing.

He kept a watchful eye on the structure for any signs of collapse. As a precaution, all teams were instructed to battle the flames from a safe distance. Doing this meant that it would take longer to put out the fire, but it was a sacrifice he was willing to make in order to ensure everyone on the crew made it home tonight.

Steam and smoke twirled and rose high into the afternoon sky, making a grey blemish on the azure backdrop. Golden flames fought back against the extinguishing teams, but slowly the steam won the battle, forcing the flames into submission. Ninety minutes later, the charred remains of the home stood in contrast to the well maintained neighborhood.

Scott took a moment to check in with his mom before making a game plan with Paige while he assisted in the clean up at the site.

"Thank you for standing guard, Mom" He gave her a kiss on the cheek. "I know it couldn't be easy to watch your house burn."

She put her palm on his face. "I knew as soon as we saw the fireball that it would be a total loss. I'm just thankful that we weren't inside." Tears started to gather in her eyes even as her face hardened. "Whoever this is has messed with the wrong family. We will not be intimidated."

Scott clenched his jaw. "What happened? I know that Rachel was the one who called it in, but can you walk me through it?"

"We were about halfway to the hospital, when I realized I had forgotten the change of clothes for your father. Second time in two days I've forgotten something."

"You're under a lot of stress with Dad. It's perfectly normal to forget things."

She gave him a sad smile. "By the time Rachel had turned us around, it had only been about twenty minutes since we had left. We turned on our street when the blast happened. I told Rachel to pull over where she was to leave room for the fire truck while I ran to the Newtons next door to make sure they got out. Thankfully, they weren't home and the only noticeable damage to their property is a few blown windows that faced our house."

He knew his mom was strong, but listening to her retell what happened and how she thought of others while the home she built over the past three decades burned to the ground sent a new wave of respect through him. He wouldn't let her down. He would figure this out.

"If you don't mind, Rachel and I are going to go to the hospital. Your father needs to know what happened. When you get the report, please keep us apprised."

"Of course. I'm going to stick around for the inspector anyway. I'll tell you as soon as I know anything."

She patted his arm and motioned for Rachel to follow her. He watched as the two walked to their truck and drove down the street.

When he turned back to his truck, Paige was leaning against the front fender, watching the crew start the long process of cleaning up hoses, equipment, and final inspection of the structure. Hampton and Gosnell walked through each room with water cans, turning over remains of walls and furniture checking for hot spots. The thought of walking through the charred rooms left a rock in his stomach.

"I'm so sorry, Scott." Paige's calm voice broke him free of the dread for a moment.

He faced her and got caught off guard by the hurt mixed with fire in her green eyes. He closed the gap between the two of them so no one could hear their conversation.

"If you wouldn't mind, I'd like to stick around until the inspector gets here. Since there was an explosion, an investigation is warranted."

"Of course. Do you want me to walk with you through the house?"

The offer warmed his heart, but as much as he wanted to keep her by his side, he wouldn't risk her safety.

"The structure hasn't been ruled stable and you don't have any gear. Just so I know you're safe, could you stay clear of the house?"

"Can you get me a radio? This way we can communicate with each other."

Scott opened the back compartment on his truck and pulled out another radio and earpiece. "Here. We can go to channel 4-08. That way we won't tie up any emergency transmissions."

She took the radio and set it to the correct channel before clipping it to her pants and placing the piece in her ear. Scott walked a few paces away, changed his channel, and put his own earpiece in place. "Let me know if you can hear this, Doc."

"Read you loud and clear, Flyboy." Her voice crackled through the radio, strong with a touch of sweetness that made his lips tip up at the corners.

"I like the sound of your voice in my ear."

"Well, I'll remind you of that the next time you grumble about me telling you what to do."

Next time. As in she would stay in New Freedom after she turned over her research. His heart stumbled over itself as the possibility took shape in his mind. "I look forward to many more next times."

The silence he received in return had him doubting his interpretation of her comment. *Way to go, Crafton.* He needed to focus on the scene before him. Paige needed time, something he could benefit from as well.

There were so many reasons he shouldn't pursue a relationship with her. First, he was her superior, which should have been enough of a reason to avoid a relationship. Given his history, Scott couldn't trust himself to not be distracted by a woman.

Although today, despite the threats against her, she stayed safe and he was able to focus on the fire, his crew, and no one was injured.

He wasn't an eighteen-year-old child anymore. He was a well trained fireman and airman. He knew how to compartmentalize.

The old mantra helped him stay focused when going through wildland fireman training and through flight school in the corps, but he was starting to doubt whether it was true or if it was simply a way for him to guard his heart from the pain of losing someone else he cared for. He turned back to check on Paige. She still stood by the truck, looking courageous and beautiful.

"I'm going to head inside to check on the clean up. You good out here?"

"I will be fine. Tell me if you see anything amiss."

"Will do." Scott placed his helmet back on his head and entered through what used to be the living room. The places that weren't covered in blackened soot were soaked with water. A few books lay on the ground in front of the bookshelf. His mother loved to read and her personal library was now gone. Scott had cleared many fires before, but the personal connection made this walk through slow his steps and constrict his lungs.

The smell of burnt fabrics and charred wood hung in the air, which added to his pool of dread. This was where he and Tylan would play games as kids and build blanket forts. It was gone. The simmering anger in his gut threatened to take over. *Compartmentalize. Focus.*

"Scott. Can you hear me?" Paige shouted into the coms.

"I hear you."

"Good. For a second there I thought you were ignoring me."

"I would never ignore you." Scott turned towards the truck. He could barely see her through the rubble. "I don't like that I can't see you."

"I can stand a bit closer to the house if you would like."

Scott visualized the property. "Stand with your back to the oak at the corner of the yard."

"Protect your blind spot," she said in a mock commanding voice.

"Right. Devil Doc has the skills."

"I've learned a thing or two from the best of the best."

"I didn't know you trained with the Air Force."

"Whatever you say, Flyboy."

Scott moved from the front of the house towards the kitchen. He wasn't a fire inspector, but given the house exploded, the kitchen was most likely the place of ignition. He stood in the doorway of the kitchen, pushing away the childhood memories of Rachel and Mom experimenting with recipes. To keep Rachel interested, Mom took recipes and taught her about the chemical reactions happening. She and Rachel used to experiment with every recipe especially in baking until they were satisfied that it was perfect. Now, the kitchen looked haunted.

"The fire inspector is approaching." The news broke Scott away from his walk down memory lane.

"I'm coming to the front." Careful not to disturb more than he already did, Scott picked his way down the hall and out the front door checking for weak spots as he went.

A man in his mid-fifties, with a scar from his right eye to his ear and a few extra pounds around his middle from working a desk job, strode toward him. Scott extended his hand in greeting and gave him a firm shake. Inspector Jones, based on his badge clipped to the left front pocket of his shirt.

"Your little town has been unfortunate as of late with the arsonist focusing here, although I do believe the last fire wasn't the same person," was the man's greeting. "It didn't quite fit the MO. I should have the test results tomorrow to confirm or deny my suspicions."

Scott's nostrils flared. He took a deep breath to remind him that this guy had no connections to this town and was here to do his job. It didn't matter that the man lacked tack as long as he was proficient at his job.

"It was reported that the house exploded. I can show you the points where the gas ran through the house. I've only cleared the bottom half of the structure, so we need to wait until my men return from the second floor."

"Thank you for being thorough. Some small town co mpanies..."

"Wow, this guy doesn't know when to stop." He could hear the eye roll in Paige's statement. Scott tuned out the inspector and focused on the voice in his ear. He didn't dare respond vocally so he settled for a head nod and brief eye contact in her direction. He could see her trying to hide a smile. He shook his head and bit his lip to keep from smiling as well.

Hampton and Gosnell came out the front at that moment and reported the problem areas on the second floor confirming where they should proceed with caution. In addition to the fire inspector, they would need a structural engineer to determine if the structure was sound or if it was a complete loss.

Paige could do that for him. "Paige, could you call the county to get a structural engineer to come out?"

"Yes. Do you have the number somewhere?"

A bit of tension left his shoulders. "You'll find it in the binder on the center console."

"Got it." Paige got into the truck and shut the door. Good, now he could focus on the walk through since she was safe.

"Let's begin, shall we?" Scott turned towards the inspector.

"I prefer silence while I work," Inspector Jones said coldly. "You can show me through, but do not speak unless I ask questions."

Scott reminded himself to remain professional. "Of course. This way."

They made their way back to the kitchen. The burn patterns on the wall and floor made it clear to him that this was the place of ignition, but he would keep his thoughts to himself since he wanted as little contact with Jones as possible.

The inspector took samples and picked through the rubble. He grunted softly then placed a melted object into an evidence bag. Sealing it, he wrote on the outside like he had done with all the other pieces of evidence that he collected. Then he started taking measurements and photographs. This was his first post-fire inspection as chief. Even though he was at the other two fires, Tucker had been the admin on duty, not him. He owed the man some coffee and a whole box full of donuts for having to deal with this guy for those two fires.

While the inspector continued to take pictures of everything, Paige came across the radio. "The engineer said that he will be out tomorrow afternoon at the earliest. He would call if he had to reschedule. I gave him yours and Paola's numbers."

"Thanks, Paige, you are a real lifesaver." His words were met with a glare from the inspector. Scott had to resist the need to roll his eyes. "We'll hopefully be done in here soon. Sit tight."

"Copy that, Flyboy. Enjoy your time with Mr. Congeniality in there." She said with a laugh.

Instead of raising the man's ire with another response, Scott simply let the comment hang between them, hoping she wouldn't take it the wrong way.

Finally, forty-five minutes later, the inspector finished his evaluation. "I'll have my preliminary results on your desk tomorrow morning with the final report as soon as all of the samples come back. That should be about five to fourteen days since the lab is a bit behind."

Scott nodded quickly, hoping to rid himself of the man as fast as he could. Once out of the house the two went their separate ways. As Scott approached the truck, all he could think of was seeing Paige and talking through everything that he saw. He may not be a fire inspector, but the gas hose to the oven looked like it was cut and the contraption the inspector bagged could have been some kind of trigger.

Scott was close enough to the truck now that he should have been able to see Paige's beautiful face through the window, but the cab was empty. He slowly turned, looking for any signs of her. It was like she had disappeared.

There on the ground next to the driver's door was a cloth. He picked it up carefully. The sickly sweet smell made his stomach drop to his knees. Chloroform. Someone had taken her. How could he let this happen again? He would not let history repeat itself.

"Hold on, Paige. We will find you." He sent an emergency text out to Rachel and Tylan. They needed to pool their resources, because he wouldn't give up until she was in his arms.

Chapter 17

P AIGE TRIED TO PUSH herself from the darkness that
held her hostage. Her eyelids refused to listen to her
commands to open. What happened? Her brain was in a
fog, wandering through random snippets of memory.

Images of the fire at the Craftons floated to the surface.
They put out the fire, but the house was probably a total
loss. Scott asked her to call the county for the structural
engineer. After getting off the phone with them, she got
out of the truck, to see if she could hear the conversation
between Scott and the Fire Investigator. Scott would have
most likely told her, but she was never one to sit idly.

Then there was a sickly sweet smell and a voice. *"You
should have listened to my orders the first time. Now you will
have no choice"*. Blackness overtook her.

They had taken her. Who were they? The voice sounded
so familiar.

Where was she? She needed to see.

Slowly, one eyelid opened, or she thought it had opened.
There was only more darkness.

Another memory flashed in her mind, "*Remember, sight is not your only sense. What do you feel? What can you hear? Is there a particular smell?*" Hank had blindfolded her and told her to describe the things on the table in front of her. At the time, she thought the exercise was childish, but now she was thankful for his training.

Paige pulled on her arms, but they were bound at her wrists and her shoulders were held against something hard. Same sensation with her legs. She was in a seated position. Tied to a chair with arms. The wood grains felt warm under her fingertips. At least it wasn't metal. Wood would be easier to break.

The air held a stale musty smell, as if she was either in a basement or old building that hadn't been used in quite some time. To her left she heard the creak of a floorboard and a muffled voice. If she were in a basement, the sound would have come from above her.

She was tied to a wooden chair in an old wood structure somewhere. Not knowing how long she was out, it was difficult to guess how far from New Freedom they were. Did they travel by car, plane, truck? She willed her brain to pull more details out, but the reel of memories was a blank screen.

The effects of the chloroform hadn't worn off completely, so she rolled her head to face the ceiling. Little pin pricks of light filtered through a fabric. A blindfold. At least she wasn't truly blind and her eyes were, indeed, still working.

She let her head roll down so her chin was on her chest. If she was going to get out of this, she needed to save her energy, but she could still listen.

Thump. Thump. Thump. Solid steps pacing somewhere. The voice of her captor she strained to hear. It was muffled, as if she was hearing it through a wall. There was only one voice that paused every so often. He was probably on the phone. What she wouldn't give to be able to actually hear what he was saying.

Click. Creak. Bang. The sudden noise made her flinch, but she needed to make her captor believe she was still unconscious so that he would speak freely in front of her.

"I already told you, she didn't have any case." They were after her research. Good thing she had already given it to Rachel. She knew it would get to Agent Wilson.

"I'll go to her place and the fire station. Those are the only two places she frequents. She must have hidden it somewhere."

Her captor's voice sounded so familiar. Why did she know that voice? His pacing stopped and he slammed his fist against something solid.

"That was *not* a part of the deal. You have the nerd now. Force her to make a new copy."

He growled low and threatening.

He huffed out a sigh. "I'll find your precious research, then I'll make her disappear."

The door slammed shut and Paige left out a whimper. She was alone, and for now she was alive. It could be the blindfold or the drugs still fogging her brain, but the solitude she had forged over the last few years was threatening to swallow her.

"We will find you." Charles' words echo in her mind as a tear traced down her cheek.

God, I'm not sure if you can hear me, but please send help. I'm alone and I can't get out of this by myself.

"I am with you wherever you go." God's words she had read long ago washed over her. Even now she was not alone, but she needed to figure out a way to stay alive long enough so that help would come.

Her captor's last words sent a shiver down her spine. She needed a plan. Pulling on her restraints, she prayed for a weak spot in the chair to show itself.

The hard plastic dug into her skin. The pain she could endure as long as she got to see Scott again. She needed to tell him how much she cared about him. Who was she kidding? She had fallen hard for the handsome fire chief with the blue eyes that made her want to tear down her own walls of self-preservation, to take a chance on love again.

The door opened so hard the windows around her all rattled. There was a porch and windows. Definitely not in a shed, but could be some other out building or a cabin. Strong, heavy footfalls made their way straight for her. She attempted to roll her head when she heard the noise, but her hope of going undetected was short lived.

"I see that the chloroform is wearing off." He grabbed her upper arm and a pinch pricked her skin. "I can't have you running off on me. I worked too hard to get you here."

His fingers ran gently down her cheek. She tried to flinch away from his touch, but whatever he gave her was taking effect already, making her reactions sluggish.

"Sleep well, partner." He patted her leg.

Marcus? The soft click of the door was the last thing she heard before slipping into the darkness again.

Scott ran his hand through his hair as he paced the short distance from one end of the command center to the other. Tylan and Rachel were typing at lightning speed across their keyboards.

How could he have let the woman that he loved be taken? Loved? Yes, if he were honest with himself, he loved her. They hadn't known each long, but she blew past every defense he had. From her emerald eyes to her feisty spirit that matched her fiery red hair, she was intelligent, stubborn, and the strongest woman he knew.

"Stop pacing, Griz. That won't bring her back," Rachel snapped. "You have two choices. You can continue to pace and drive us all crazy, or you can use that brain of yours and come up with a plan to get back the woman that you love."

Scott stopped pacing and stared at his sister. He never said out loud anything about his feelings towards Paige.

Since when did his sister, who missed social cues her whole childhood, learn to be so perceptive of others?

Rachel rolled her eyes. "I wanted to be able to read others like normal people did." She sighed. "For years, Mom patiently took me to a mall or park everyday to people watch. She would sit with me as I tried over and over again to understand people's facial features, voice inflections, and posture. Sarcasm was the hardest to understand, but I've found I enjoy using it. It gives others the illusion that I'm not some kind of freak calculating and gathering information from their every move."

He tilted his head. "Being normal is overrated. Besides 'calculating and gathering information' of someone else's moves is what a good profiler does. Very little gets past the trained eye."

One side of Rachel's mouth slid up. "Mom said that she was a profiler. It's how she and Dad met. She was brought in to find him. Little did she know, he would be the one to save her."

Huh. Respect for his mother grew even more. He should have asked her more questions when growing up.

He could hear more of that story later. Now, he needed to focus on finding the woman who captured his heart.

He needed a plan. He was an airman and the son of Charles Crafton.

He dialed his mother.

"Scott, did you find her?" His mother's voice sounded focused. No need for pleasantries when someone was missing.

"Not yet." He gritted his teeth.

"You will. I believe in you." Her words gave him hope.

"Is Dad awake? We could use some of his insight."

"He is awake and alert at the moment."

Scott put the phone on speaker as his dad's voice filled the space.

"What do you need to know?"

A lot of things, but he would settle for a clue of any sort to find Paige. "We are going back through your notes trying to figure out the identity of Eros. If we can track him, then we might be able to find Paige."

Tylan looked up from his screen. "I've attempted to make a list of the people who moved here after Paige arrived on the assumption that they followed her here."

"Who's on your list?" Charles asked.

"Ian Wilson, the new mechanic at Dale's automotive; Bella Viruel, a new nurse at the hospital; Kevin Jones, he works from home on his computer and volunteers for the FD; Marcus Newberg, Paige's partner and owner of a moving company; and Maris DeCastro, who works in real estate and volunteers at the animal shelter."

"We were looking for someone who moved here after Paige, but also held a job or volunteer work that gave them esteem within the community," Rachel added.

"This would allow them to hide in plain sight behind their good deeds. People don't tend to question those who are known to do good," Paola agreed.

Now that he knew more of her past, his mother even sounded like a profiler.

"I can't think of anyone else to add to the list with those parameters," Tylan added.

"You can remove Bella from your list. I just saw her in the cafeteria. She couldn't have taken Paige," Paola stated.

"Maris DeCastro you could remove too," Dad said. "Paige said that it was a man who attempted to take her at the hospital."

"But that could have been a grunt," Tylan suggested.

"No, I agree. Paige said that she called him out for being Eros and he applauded her." Disgust roiled in his gut.

"So Marcus, Kevin, or Ian." Tylan ticked off on his fingers.

Scott took out his fire company phone. Opening the dispatching app he used his administration access to check to see who was checked in for the day and their status.

"Kevin switched shifts and was on a medical call when Paige was taken. Let me call his partner and confirm their status."

The phone only rang twice before Kevin's partner for the day, Daren Colson answered.

"Colson."

"Colson, its Chief Crafton."

"Yes, sir." There was trepidation in his voice.

"When did you and Jones complete your call to 45 E. Main Street?"

"1300. The patient is a lonely widow who likes to bend the ear of whoever gets the misfortune of being on the receiving end of her call," he responded without hesitation.

1300 was after Paige was taken. "Thank you, Colson. Stay safe out there."

"Will do, sir."

Scott shoved the phone in his pocket. "Jones was with his partner on a call until after Paige was taken. That leaves Marcus or Ian. Two are better than five."

"If Ian was working today, his whereabouts should be easy to track. I'll call Dale's and see if the man is there." Tylan pulled out his phone and stepped away to make the call.

"What do we know about Marcus?" Scott asked.

"Not much. He volunteers on the same shift as Paige and was assigned as her partner after his training rides were completed," Rachel offered.

"How do you know that?"

Rachel shrugged. "Paige and I talk. You know, girl stuff and things."

Scott gave her a pointed look.

"Fine. I tried my best to do the best friend thing at first, but Paige is different. She gets me. What started as practice in making friends and reading people turned into an actual friendship. You may have feelings for her, but you're not the only one hoping she is alright."

Scott's heart squeezed. Apparently, it was still difficult for his sister to make friends which, made his resolve to find Paige grow even stronger. He needed to steer the conversation back to figuring out who took her.

"Marcus owns a moving company, right?" A detail clicked in his brain. "Can you bring up those newspaper reports about the stolen art?"

"Scott, we are going to go," Paola interrupted. "All this thinking has drained your father."

"I don't need to rest." The slowing of his father's words suggested otherwise.

"Bring her home, Scott. I know you can do this."

His mother's words infused him with strength. "I will."

Rachel threw the articles up on the big screen. He scanned each of them.

"There. Three of these articles say that they noticed the missing art after they moved. Each time, the moving company had to store the belongings due to a delay in the buying process."

It wasn't solid evidence, but it was a workable theory. They weren't looking for something to stand up in court, they just needed to find Paige before she disappeared.

"You don't happen to know where Marcus lives, do you?"

Rachel shook her head. "Paige didn't share more than what she and Marcus did at the station. I'm not even sure she knew. I think once she called him a womanizer and said he could charm just about any woman into going on a date with him."

Scott's heart stuttered. "She did?"

Rachel snorted. "No way. Paige saw him for what he was. A shallow man that wanted no commitment. Besides, she *had* sworn off men. Until you burst into her life."

Scott couldn't ignore Rachel's use of the past tense. He and Paige had things they needed to figure out together.

"I can text Mateo to see if he knows where Marcus lives or where the moving company's office is located."

Scott snapped his fingers. "Mateo is still on light duty from his concussion. Be careful, though, we don't want to put him in more danger than he already put himself in by reporting what he heard in that warehouse. Wait."

Rachel jerked her head up.

"Ask him about where the warehouse is located, too. I don't think there will be stolen goods in there, but the things stored there could be targeted, which means we could catch them in the act of stealing."

Not the charges he was hoping to nail the man with, but it would at least get him off the streets. He would need to call Harry Turvet when they had the address. He could handle watching the place.

Tylan strode back over. "Dale confirms that Ian was at work all day today. He didn't take his lunch until 1330. He apparently drew the short straw to go last."

"That means that Marcus is the only one left on our list." Scott could feel the adrenaline rising. They needed to find Marcus. He only prayed that they weren't missing something.

An alarm rang from Rachel's computer. She punched a few keys and threw the camera feeds up on the center screen.

"There." Rachel enlarged a camera feed trained on the area around Paige's trailer. A figure moved towards the door of her trailer, careful not to look at the camera.

"Tylan, ready to get some answers?" Scott strode toward the supply closet. "We'll take the UTV part way and approach on foot."

Tylan squared his shoulders and gave him a curt nod. Scott grabbed two sets of comms and an additional mag for his gun strapped to his side.

"Rachel, be our eyes."

Rachel put a hand on his arm. "Bring him back alive. He needs to tell us where Paige is."

The man preyed on women and others. He represented the evil in this world that Scott fought against during his time overseas. He had enough death and destruction.

He gave her a curt nod. "I will leave the vengeance to the Lord."

Scott and Tylan took the UTV about halfway to Paige's trailer on the south side of the property. While making their way they talked strategy on how to broach the dwelling.

Rachel interrupted their planning, "The guy is running. I'm not sure if he heard you or if he found what he was looking for and fled."

"New plan. UTV will cover the ground faster." Scott pushed the accelerator the whole way. "Rachel, which way is he headed?"

"He's headed towards the service road between our property and the state forest land."

They needed to head the intruder off before he crossed the property line.

Rachel's agitated huff sounded over the comms. "He just passed our last posted camera. I don't have eyes on him anymore."

Tylan grabbed the roll bar above his head as they flew over the ruts in the path. He knew that he should slow down, but he couldn't help feel that this was their only shot at getting Paige back.

Finally the thick forest stopped abruptly as they soared onto the service road. An engine roared as a dirt bike flew past them. Scott let out a tortured scream as the UTV skidded to a stop.

The intruder sped away, taking the hope of finding Paige with him.

Chapter 18

S COTT THREW THE UTV into park and stumbled towards the back of the shed. He hit his knees, letting the cool, damp soil soak through his pants. Lifting his face to the tree cover and heavens above, the cry rose in his throat, cutting off his ability to think. That was their best lead and he let it slip through his fingers.

"God, I can't do this." A tear slid down his cheek. "I need help. Show us where she is. I need to tell her how I feel. Please, Lord."

The prayer wasn't the most eloquent thing he had spoken, but it was all he could do in this moment. God knew the cry of his heart.

"We are going to find her." Tylan put a hand on his shoulder.

Scott rose slowly to his feet. "Let's go see if Rachel has anything from Mateo yet."

Coming through the doors to the command center, they caught the end of Rachel's phone conversation.

"Alright, thank you. Please let me know if there is any activity there."

Scott tilted his head, but before he could ask, Rachel filled them in. "I thought I would multitask. While you two raced across the property, I called Officer Turvet to let him know about the warehouse. He said the best he could do is ask for a unit to drive by every hour or two, but if he heard anything that could help us across the scanner, he would tell us."

"I guess that means that Mateo texted you back. Did he give you an address for Marcus' home or office?"

"He doesn't know where the man lives. I'm not convinced that Marcus shares that with anyone, but the office for the moving company is in Oxford."

That was the next largest town about twenty-five miles north, off Highway 15 just past the state forest land that bordered his family's property.

Scott was trying to figure out who should go check out the office. Tylan and he couldn't go because they were both on duty. He didn't want to send Rachel. She had proven that she was more than capable of defending herself, but the big brother in him couldn't bring himself to send her straight into the lion's den.

Rachel interrupted his thought process. "Marcus is highly intelligent. There is no way he would leave something incriminating at the legitimate side of his business."

Another dead end?

This is why Scott never became a cop. He wouldn't be able to deal with all of the roads that led to nowhere. Firefighting was better. Read the fire. Make a plan of action. Execute the plan. When the fire changes, you adapt. Scott stilled.

"Rachel, is there anything in Dad's notes about how Heather communicates with others in the organization?"

If they couldn't find Marcus through the smoke screen of life on the right side of the law, then they would have to peer on the other side of the smoke to find him.

Rachel's eyes pinged back and forth as she scrolled through the notes. "Looks like they either communicated via text or an online chat room. I have an idea. It's a long shot and I'm going to need help."

Tylan's phone went off. "I've got to go. There is a MVC in town. I'll be back as soon as possible."

When Scott turned his attention back to Rachel, she was texting on her phone. "Help will be here in about twenty minutes."

"Who did you..."

"Mateo is one of the best hackers that I know. He also has a personal stake in bringing this man down."

She had a point. "Has he been here before?"

"Only upstairs. I'll escort him down when he gets here."

"No, I'll do it." Scott pinned her with a stare. "What is your idea?"

"Marcus is accused of selling women and other merchandise online. I'm going to find his auction site. Hopefully before he moves his current holdings."

His sister's cold rendering of the despicable things Marcus did turned his stomach sour, but he understood why she took a cold detachment. It was hard to think of Paige captured and possibly being sold.

He swallowed hard. "What do you need me to do?"

Rachel's face went blank. "Pray we find her in time. And call Agent Wilson." Rachel handed him a business card. "He might be able to get us access to things to help us find her faster."

Finally, something he could do. Scott strode up the steps to watch for Mateo and inform Wilson what was happening. Before he could place the call, he received a text from Kevin Jones.

Chief, thought you should know that Newberg just left the station.

Saw him going through MacFarland's locker.

Wouldn't say what he was looking for, just that she asked him to look for something for her.

Thanks for the heads up. Scott texted back.

Hope bloomed in his chest. Marcus was in the area looking for something of Paige's. It meant that she was most likely close by.

Scott hit the call button.

"This is Agent Wilson."

"Agent Wilson, this is the Fire Chief in New Freedom, Scott Crafton. I need your help. Paige MacFarland has been taken."

"Give me your location. I'll be there as fast as I can."

Scott gave him their location and hung up as a small SUV pulled up to the cabin. Mateo jumped out of the driver seat and bounded up the porch. Before he could knock, Scott opened the door.

To his credit Mateo didn't shrink away from Scott's stare.

"The only reason you are here right now is because my sister trusts you." Scott narrowed his eyes. "Don't betray that trust."

Mateo stood straighter and flexed his jaw. "I would never betray Rachel or your family. Besides, Paige is one of us, and if I can do something to find her, then I will."

Scott held his gaze a moment longer, then motioned for Mateo to follow him.

"I understand that you haven't been to the bunker yet." They descended the stairs. "My family runs an organization that helps find people who are lost." Scott paused and looked over his shoulder. "You cannot tell anyone where we are located or what you see inside. Some of the people we help are running from danger and we need to keep their identity secret as well as our own."

If Mateo was surprised by the declaration, he hid his shock well. "Like I said, I would never betray your family."

Scott opened the door. "Welcome to the Kora command center."

"Whoa," Mateo said in a breathy voice.

Scott chuckled. "You didn't even see the armory yet."

"Mateo, I'm glad you're here." Rachel marched over and grabbed the poor boy's hand. Dragging him across the room, she signaled him to sit at the conference table. "We need to find an auction site on the dark web."

Snapping out of his wonder and focusing on the work ahead of him, Mateo took his laptop out of his bag. "What are they auctioning?"

"Paige and possibly her research as well. Although I'm fairly certain they were hired to steal the program for someone specific. It was a God thing that Paige handed over the program to her superiors this morning."

Rachel's blunt words made the color drain from Mateo's face before he regained his composure and they got to work.

Scott needed something to do, but without intel riding around town looking for her would be pointless. Scott moved towards a smaller screen off to the right with the evidence board displayed on it.

"Rachel, can you put an area map up here for me?"

A moment later, a map appeared. Scott used the stylus on the counter and drew on the map. He put a dot on the office for Marcus' moving company, the fire station, and the warehouse. The points that they knew Marcus was known to be on a regular basis. The warehouse and office were both in Oxford. So why would he volunteer in New Freedom? He must have been targeting Paige from the moment he arrived.

Scott zoomed in on Oxford. It was a larger town than New Freedom, but still not truly a city. It would be easy enough to hide in plain sight though.

"Where are you, Paige?"

A soft moan escaped past her lips as she mentally pushed back the darkness. Again.

Her arms were bound behind her back as she lay on something that scratched her skin and smelled of must. Somehow, she was moved from the chair to some kind of mattress. She tried to roll over and sit up. The movement made her want to close her eyes and slip back into oblivion.

Peeling her eyes open, a dark room came into focus. No blindfold. That meant they didn't care if she saw their faces. So she was either going to be killed or shipped off to some place where there was no coming back. Given the two choices, she much rather live in paradise than in hell on earth, but she would let that fate up to God.

If this whole situation taught her one thing, it was that she was not alone. Twice now, God had Scott show up to save her. He was with her. She wasn't alone.

"She awakes," a dark voice spoke from across the room. The voice didn't belong to Marcus. How could she have missed that Marcus was this evil?

"Who are you?" Her voice rasped, weakened by the drugs lingering in her system.

"Malinoe wants you to look good for the pictures. Hunter says he wants you to disappear. Good thing for him, we make women disappear without too much bloodshed."

A shiver ran down her spine. She wished that there would be some kind of light. The curtains were drawn and none of the lights were on. She would have to continue to rely on her other senses.

Improvise. Adapt. Overcome. She could do this. She could stay alive long enough for help to arrive.

A bag dropped next to her on the bed.

"What is this?"

"Some things to make your face look better for the camera," the voice seethed.

"How am I supposed to make my face look better with my hands behind my back?"

A strong hand gripped her arm and hoisted her off the bed. She stumbled forward, but the man pulled her back to straighten her out.

"Be careful there, sweetheart, can't have you break your nose."

The pressure on her shoulders released as the zip ties fell to the floor. She cradled her wrist where they were rubbed raw until he shoved the bag into her arms.

"You have ten minutes to make yourself look good."

"What if I choose not to?" She wanted to know what this guy was willing to do.

"It's simple. Follow directions and don't try anything stupid and we won't take your pretty friend, Rachel, too. She is a beauty even covered in mud."

Paige narrowed her eyes wishing she could see any detail about the man.

"You were in the SUV."

"Very good," he said in a condescending voice. "Now go." He shoved her through a doorway. She slammed into what felt like a sink. The man reached in and closed the door, turning on the light as he did, blinding her temporarily.

Paige slowly blinked to help her eyes adjust to the light. Regaining her sight, she found herself staring into a filthy mirror with a crack along its top corner. The sink was stained but otherwise fairly clean like it had been used recently. There was only a tiny window above the toilet that looked neglected and a miracle if it worked. She wouldn't be able to fit through the window even if the toilet could hold her weight.

Her eyes looked haunted. Dark circles and stress lines formed around them, causing them to appear sullen. She could use a long soak in a warm bath and actual sleep in her own bed. It was only then that she noticed someone had changed her clothes. She was no longer wearing her t-shirt and jeans, but a cocktail dress that hugged all of her curves, what few of them she had. She tried not to think about who had done that task. She didn't feel any pain in that area of her body, so she should count her blessings there.

"Please, God. Protect me." A tear rolled down her cheek. She swiped it away. There was no time for crying. She only had ten minutes or they'd take Rachel.

She rotated her shoulders and tried to stretch out the stiffness that had settled there from being bound. Unzipping the bag, she peered inside. Makeup, a hairbrush, some dry shampoo, and styling mousse filled the compartment. This was clearly put together by a woman. She only hoped that the woman who put this together was the one who changed her.

Paige took as much time as she could getting ready. No reason to rush. The longer she could give Scott to find her the better, but she also didn't want them to follow through on their threat against Rachel.

The pounding on the door made her jump. "Two more minutes."

She looked at herself again in the mirror. It was amazing what a little concealer and a brush could do to bring a person's appearance back to life.

Now, if only she could figure out how to arm herself. She shuffled through the bag. Only sponges, brushes, and makeup containers. If she could possibly break one of the brushes, she might be able to get a sharp enough edge to defend herself.

The light went off and she was pitched into darkness again. She was going to sleep with the lights on for a while after this.

"Time's up." The door banged against the wall and the same strong hand grabbed her by the arm and drug her into the open room.

There was a ring light on a stand in front of a blank wall. It didn't give off enough light to see much of her surroundings or her captor, but at least it wasn't completely dark any more.

Like an ogre being forged out of the dark depths of middle earth, Marcus emerged from the shadows. The ring light cast harsh lines across his face, giving him a menacing air. His friendly, flirty looks were long gone, replaced by a viciousness that made Paige pull back.

"Surprised, partner?"

Paige wanted to punch the smug smile off of his face. "Why do you do this?"

"Not many women can refuse my charms, but mostly it's for the money. It's a shame, really. I was beginning to enjoy your intellect, yet for as smart as you may be, you still didn't figure it out. Shame. Because there is no way that all brawn and no brains fire chief can figure out where you are. He'll have to live with the regret that two women in his charge disappeared into the night."

Paige rose to her full height and raised her chin.

"You have no idea what Scott is capable of. I know he'll find me."

"No one will find you once you leave this cabin." Marcus leaned so close to her face she had nowhere to look except his dark eyes. "No one."

How could she have ever thought him innocent? No matter how malicious he looked, she would not give him the satisfaction of seeing her squirm.

He stepped back and roamed over her body in the ridiculous outfit. "I knew you had curves hidden under that uniform, but"— he gave a low whistle — "we should get a good profit for you. Add in that brain of yours, and it will definitely be a good day on the market for us."

Disgust wasn't even a strong enough word that she had for her former partner.

"You better," the mystery man who never stood in the light said. "Malinoe isn't happy that you lost the research."

Marcus snorted. "Not my fault Hunter told her to give it to another agent. So unless you want to kill a federal agent, then you best help me turn a hefty profit tonight."

It was little comfort to know that Marcus probably wouldn't kill her, only sell her to the highest bidder.

"Alright, partner, stand in the light and do as I say. We need good shots to draw in the deeper pockets."

Paige moved to stand in front of the wall. "I am not your partner," she growled.

Marcus ran his finger down her bare arm. "You only wish you could be my partner. If only I could break you. Sadly, I believe that you'd rather die than join me."

She held his gaze. "You'd be right."

"Capture that fire. Oh yes, I know of a few men who would be interested in that spirit."

She wanted to glare more but didn't want to feed their delusions. Marcus barked instructions at her while the mystery man took a few more pictures. This was by far the most humiliating thing she had ever done.

Buy time. *They will find me. They will find me.* She repeated the words until they were the only thing she focused on. *Please, God, let them find me.*

"I think we have enough. I'm going to work on sending out the invitations. Put her back in the chair."

Marcus walked out a door where Paige could see that the sun was almost completely set. It would be night soon. Which meant more darkness. The ring light went out and a strong hand grabbed her.

On instinct Paige swung out and connected with a solid wall of muscle.

"I wouldn't try anything stupid, or we'll have a second prize tonight," mystery man snarled.

Paige stilled at his threat against Rachel.

"That's better. Now sit." He forced her into the seat. Taking no time to be gentle, he tied her to the chair, zipty-ing on her wrists and ankles to the chair. The wounds on her joints burned under the new restraints.

The mystery man's breath tickled her cheek. "He's right about one thing. You will do well."

Paige swallowed. *God, please don't leave me now. Help Scott find me.*

Chapter 19

A GENT WILSON HAD ARRIVED. The distraction allowed Scott the opportunity to run through everything that they knew so far about Newberg, a.k.a Eros.

"You are positive that Marcus Newberg is Eros?" the agent asked.

"The evidence is circumstantial at best, but I don't need this to stand up in court." Scott pushed the desperation back down." I need to find Paige."

"But I need it to hold up in court. We need to gather hard evidence to put him away for good."

"When we find Paige, you'll have a witness." Irritation quickly replaced the dread. "If God sees fit, we'll catch him in the act."

"Let's pray that He does. Do you have any clue where he is keeping her?"

Scott walked towards the map he had on the screen. "We've had two sightings of the man in the area since he took her, which means he needs to be close by."

"He'll want a place that is isolated. Someplace where no one would accidentally stumble onto them or overhear them from a distance." Wilson scanned the map.

Scott looked at the map again. "The fire station, warehouse, and office are all places that he frequents in his public life."

"What about this forested area?" Wilson pointed. "Does he have any claims in there?"

"The state forest has a few hunting cabins that belong to long established families of the community. I doubt he would have access to one. Although he is a con artist at heart, so it wouldn't be out of the realm of possibility that he talked someone into allowing him to use one."

"I need to make a call." Wilson started to walk away. "We need to get eyes on those cabins. Something tells me that's where they are."

A piercing alarm shrilled through the space and the wall of screens went blank.

"Rachel, what's going on?" Scott commanded himself to breathe. Just when they were making some progress, this happened. Whatever this was.

"No time to explain, Griz. Mateo, I need you tethered. Four hands are faster than two." Rachel bent closer to the screen as if her death stare alone could fend off the incoming attack.

With each passing second, Scott's grip on the table in front of him grew tighter. He knew it was a matter of time before they tried again. The car accident, the house explosion, now the hacking. Someone was trying to get them to back off, which meant that they were probably closer to the truth than they realized.

The screens in front of him jumped to life as Rachel gave a victory shout.

"Now let's see who tried to best our system." Rachel's face held no emotion as her fingers flew across the keys. "Where are you?"

"Stop." Mateo pointed at the screen. To Scott it looked like all the other jumbled numbers and letters that were streaming past.

"It looks like a bunch of numbers and letters to me," he mumbled.

Rachel looked at him with agitation. "It looks like an IP address. At least this first part, anyway."

"I'm on it." Mateo took his computer back to his original seat. Scott might need to take a few lessons from Paige once this was all over. He felt helpless, something he hadn't felt since Heather had disappeared.

"This, though, doesn't look like computer code." Rachel tilted her head as if a different angle would make the numbers make sense.

Scott peered over her shoulder. "That's because it is map coordinates." He took his phone and brought up the map app. They didn't have the decimals to the furthest degree, but it was enough to get them close. The map app zoomed in over the southern part of the state forest. Scott drew a circle around the area of the forest on the map he had already marked up.

"Got it." Mateo turned his computer. "It's the site for the auction."

"How do you know that?" Scott barked.

Mateo drew his eyes downward. "There were pictures," he said in a small voice.

Scott's blood began to boil. "Let me see those pictures."

"No time to go all caveman." Rachel halted his progress. "We need to try and find a backdoor to the site to shut it down. You focus on finding where they are holding her. I don't think whoever hacked us was trying to harm us. I think they were sending us a message."

"Why do you say that?" Agent Wilson voiced Scott's own question.

"They gave up too easily. Someone with the skills to get through the first layer of our system wouldn't give up as quickly as this person did. I think they wanted us to find the auction site and location." Rachel paused for a moment, then looked straight at Scott. "I think it was Heather trying to help us."

"A bit unconventional, but hacking someone wouldn't leave any red flags in her world." It pained Scott to even say that last part.

Rachel moved to stand in front of him. "She chose to stay and fight. She is a smart and creative woman. She knows what she's doing."

"I'm not sure who you're talking about, but if she helped us get MacFarland back, then she seems to be on our side," Wilson interjected.

"Do you have eyes yet?" Scott turned from his sister to address the DCIS agent.

"It should be coming up on my laptop now."

"May I?" Rachel pointed to the computer. Wilson made no effort to let Rachel take the device. "I only want to put it up on one of our screens so we have a better picture."

"Fine." Wilson fixed her with a stare. "I will be watching you."

For once Rachel kept her comments to herself. Scott thanked the Lord for small mercies. Couldn't Wilson see that they all wanted Paige back and in one piece? As an officer of the law, he might find some of their tactics unconventional, so maybe Scott should cut him a break.

Wilson spoke to the operator controlling the satellite, relaying the coordinates they discovered in Heather's message. The cameras zoomed in on the forested area. By Scott's count, there were three cabins tucked into the trees in this area. None of them had smoke coming from the chimneys or lights on inside.

"What about thermal imaging?" Scott asked. "We could zoom in on each of the three cabins and see if there were any heat signatures."

Wilson grunted his agreement and gave the directions to the operator. The first cabin came into sharp focus, but no heat signatures were detected. Not even small rodents. The second cabin told a similar story. No one had been at these cabins for quite some time. It would be the perfect spot to hide.

The last cabin was the furthest from the road, tucked along a stream. It would give a buffer of sound even though they hadn't had as much rain as usual for this time of year.

Scott let the short prayer slip from his lips. "Lord, let her be here."

"Amen," Rachel and Mateo said together.

They all had their eyes glued to the screen as the cabin came into focus. There were three heat signatures and one vehicle that was registering heat.

"We know where they are holding her." Scott tore his eyes off the screen to face Mateo. "Have you been able to stop that auction?"

Mateo shook his head. "I'm almost...there. I'm in."

With a few more skilled strokes the site before him went blank.

"What happened?" Scott bellowed.

"Relax. That was me." Then Mateo started to type. *Kora: This auction has now ended. We know who you are and where you're hiding. We have eyes everywhere, so don't even think about running.*

"Someone has watched too much TV. This isn't going to work," Wilson said with an exasperated sigh.

The screen flickered a moment before a message was written back. *Malinoe: You have no idea who you are dealing with. Now you'll have to watch her burn.*

The screen went black again. "Mateo? Please tell me that was you." The dread pooled in Scott's stomach.

Mateo's head hung. "Sorry, I lost the connection."

"Understood." Wilson disconnected his call and addressed the rest of the group. "Our satellite time is running out."

"We need to keep an eye on the cabin until we can get our own eyes on the place."

Scott opened his mouth to continue, but Rachel cut off his tirade. "We can use the drones. Now that we know the location of the cabin, we can use our own eyes."

Rachel marched over to the supply closet-turned-armory. She spun to face Mateo, who was following behind her. "Don't touch anything."

He nodded his head quickly in compliance. The poor kid had it bad for his sister. Scott wasn't sure if Rachel even noticed. She surprised him about her knowledge of his feelings for Paige, though. He gave himself a mental shake. Mateo and Rachel were a problem for another day.

Rachel unlocked one of the lower cabinets in the back and brought out a briefcase. She grabbed four sets of comms on her way out past a stunned Mateo.

"Come on, Mateo. I promise to give you a proper tour after we find Paige." That seemed to snap Mateo out of his daze. Scott grabbed a S&W 40 handgun and an extra mag.

"There are two drones in the case. We can use both, but we need to get closer."

"We can take the UTVs. It will be faster to travel the trails across our land than to go miles out of the way to use the highway." A plan started to form in Scott's mind. "We'll drop you and Mateo at our property line. You get the drones in the air and guide Wilson and myself in."

He extended the butt of the gun toward Mateo, but he raised his hands in surrender. "I don't do guns. My father was gunned down in front of me and I vowed never to touch one."

They didn't have time for Mateo to work through his past. Rachel grabbed the gun and mag from his hand. "I'll protect us. Let's go."

"No!" Marcus threw the computer across the room, shattering the screen and breaking the hinges.

Paige flinched but let a smile creep up her lips. "Having computer problems?"

She probably should have held her tongue, but she couldn't help it. Whatever had happened, Scott and Rachel were behind it. She knew it.

Marcus spun to face her with fists at his side, nostrils flared and his shoulders heaving. "Your friends just signed your death wish, and quite possibly mine as well."

He crossed the room in four long strides. Paige kept her chin held high as he approached. She would not be intimidated. He grabbed a fist full of her hair lighting her scalp with pain. She fought the tears that wanted to fall. Taking a few hard breaths through her nose, she stared down the man who she had trusted to help her save lives.

"I thought you were like me. One who doesn't destroy lives. One who saves them." Something flickered in his eyes. Regret. It was then that she knew he didn't want to kill her.

Before she could play on the bond they had, his eyes turned to stone. "You have no idea who you are dealing with. Malinoe's reach is vast and they will not stop until you all are no longer a threat."

"Duly noted," she seethed through her teeth.

Marcus threw her head back as he released her hair, causing the chair to tip backwards slightly with the force. The chair thankfully stayed upright, but the pain in her scalp radiated down her neck and across her shoulders.

The front door flew open and the mystery man strode across the threshold, hood in place looking like a reaper. All he needed was a scythe. Instead he held a blow torch in his hand. Pyroeis. She still couldn't see the man's face, but she at least knew he was close by. For now anyway.

"So nice of you to join us, Pyroeis."

Not taking the bait and moving close to her, the man turned to Marcus. "You know what needs to be done."

"I may be many things, but a murderer is not one of them." Marcus stood inches from Pyroeis, daring the man to change his mind.

Pyroeis sneered. "Malinoe was right. You are weak."

Using the torch gun in one quick motion, he knocked Marcus over the head. Marcus crumbled to the ground with a thump.

"Such a waste of talent on a boy with no backbone." Pyroeis sounded almost disappointed in Marcus.

"You won't get away with this." Paige put as much confidence behind her threat as she could. If Scott and Rachel had figured out the auction site, then they could be on their way now. She had no idea where *here* was, exactly, but she would hold on to that hope until her dying breath.

"I will. But don't worry, fire is a beautiful thing. The way it consumes every living thing in its way, choking out life until nothing remains." The awe in his voice when he spoke of fire sent a shiver through her.

Prodding the madman may not be a wise choice, but she needed to buy as much time as possible. "I much prefer a forest after a fire, when new life begins again in the fertile soil. See the fire clears the ground of thorns and thickets to let the new trees grow. God brings beauty from the ashes."

God did bring beauty from ashes and He had been working on making her life beautiful again after the burned mess that she walked away from overseas. She had tried hiding in the ashes of her past, not willing to let anyone in, but God had better plans for her. Ones that included friends who accepted her as family, a quiet mountain town away from the stress of the politics of DC, and a handsome fire chief whom she knew was coming for her right now.

"God has nothing to do with it," he roared, bringing Paige back from her thoughts. "Fire is what cleanses the earth of all wrongdoing. And fire will get rid of you and that sorry excuse for a man over there."

Paige flinched at his outburst.

"Don't worry, the smoke will choke the life from your lungs before the flames wash over your body." Even though she couldn't see his eyes, she felt them on her. "You won't feel a thing."

He fled the cabin with angry footsteps, slamming the door on his way out. The door bounced against the frame and stood ajar. Paige hung her head. At least he didn't set the cabin on fire yet. Maybe she had distracted him with her talk of fire and God. She would take any reprieve and precious time she could get.

She needed to get out of this chair. "Marcus," she shouted. "Marcus, get up."

Rocking forward on her feet, she attempted to stand while tied to the chair, a feat that was difficult at best. Rotating her hips, she plopped the chair down. She had moved a few inches toward Marcus and the door. At this rate she would never outrun a fire.

"Marcus," she called. "I need your help. I know that you were the one to kidnap me, but if you don't wake up, you're going to die right along with me."

Nothing. Paige watched, but she couldn't see any rise and fall of his chest. She needed to get to him. Call her crazy, but if someone was in need, she had this drive to help them. Even if they were the one who put her in this situation.

She attempted her stand and pivot maneuver again. This time when she set the chair back down, she tilted to the side. She willed the chair to right itself. Since she was bound at the shoulders to the backing and her wrists to the arms, there was nothing she could do to reverse the momentum of her fall.

She hit the ground with a thud. Pain shot through her shoulder and she winced. "Good job, Paige. Now you are on the floor," she mocked herself.

Giving up on the notion of arousing Marcus for the moment, she looked around the room for something that she could use to free herself. From her vantage point, she couldn't see much of the space. Nothing stood out to her as being helpful. She needed out of these bonds. If Pyroeis was coming back to set the place on fire, she needed to be free so she could escape.

Pulling on the restraints, she clenched her jaw and let out a guttural cry. The arm of the chair on the ground moved under the strain, which halted her angry outburst. If she could get on her back, she might have enough leverage to pull the arm away and get one hand free.

Using her hips to rock the chair back and forth, she was able to lift the chair almost far enough. When she came crashing back down on her side again, she let out a moan as her shoulder made hard contact with the floor. She would not give up. She could do this. She had to do this.

She started to rock the chair again. When she thought she had enough momentum, she went for the biggest push she could muster. The chair teetered on its side until it came down with a thud. She stared straight above, never so thankful as to be staring at old rafters and cobwebs.

Lifting her head to see the arm of the chair, she gripped it with her fingers and tried wiggling it. She dug her fingers in harder. The pain was temporary and drove her to push harder. The crack of wood lifted a satisfying grin on her face. With as much strength as she could muster, she broke the arm. Not quite what she was imagining, but her forearm was free. Sort of.

She brought her wrist over to her other hand and worked the piece of wood that still brandished a nail over the plastic tie. She sat heaving a few breaths. "You can do this Paige. Just take the sharp end of the wood and cut yourself free."

Using the embedded nail, she started to saw at the rope around her shoulders.

A soft crackle and distinct smell of wood smoke pierced her concentration. She scanned the room but couldn't see any flames. He must have set the forest on fire.

"God, if you are sending help, now would be a great time." She returned to sawing at her rope when Charles' voice filled her mind. *We will find you.*

"I know," she whispered into the room.

Chapter 20

A GENT WILSON GRIPPED THE roll bar above him as Scott flew over the trails towards the state forest land. *We're coming, Paige. Please stay alive.* The whispered desires of his heart tried to clog his throat. He pushed the emotion down using it to focus on the trail. He wanted to get there fast, but putting them in a ditch would slow them down.

Scott stopped at the sight of the sign indicating where the state forest land began.

"What is that smell?" Agent Wilson stood beside the UTV.

Smoke. It was a smell any wildland firefighter would know. One that haunted your waking hours and your dreams when you closed your eyes. It's what killed more firefighters than the flames themselves.

"We need eyes on that fire." Scott tried to believe that they weren't too late. That the fire wasn't the cabin engulfed in flames, but an unattended campfire sparking a wildfire. Rummaging through the jump bag, he threw on a pair of fire pants and flame retardant jacket. He put a pair of fireman gloves into his belt and a shake and bake emergency shelter into one of his cargo pockets. There was only one set of fire gear, but it would protect him and he would protect Paige if it came to it.

Rachel and Mateo had both drones in the air by the time he was done grabbing some other emergency supplies from the bag. He wasn't sure what he would find, but having specific supplies on his person could be the difference of surviving or not.

"We've got a visual on the cabin. There are only two heat signatures in the cabin, both lying prone on the ground."

A rock settled in his stomach. He needed to get to her. There was no way to know if she was injured or worse.

"Wait. One of them is moving." Those words spurred the desire to move. He prayed that she was the one moving, that she was still alive.

"Get me eyes on the fire and surrounding area." He would have to get as good a read on the fire as he could before heading towards the cabin.

Standing behind Mateo, he watched the drone scan the forest around the cabin and approach the blaze. Despite the early summer temperatures, they hadn't received the rains that they normally would have this time in the year. The flames easily consumed the dead leaves of last fall and dormant brush from the winter. When the sap from the pine trees around the flames ignited, the fire would spread quickly. As if his thought could make it so, the first pine tree burst into flames, causing the brush fire to explode into an all consuming inferno.

"We need to get them out of there. The wind is blowing the flames right towards them. Fly up, Mateo," Scott commanded. "There. The lake will act as a natural barrier to the west. We need to create a fire line here and here." He pointed to the screen.

Scott looked at Rachel. Mateo, who was still recovering from his concussion, and Agent Wilson decked out in his suit. "We're going to need reinforcements."

"This is state forest land, not New Freedom. Unless the rangers give us permission we technically can't take command of this fire," Rachel reminded him.

"I know. I have a few favors I'm calling in." Scott walked over to the UTV and started to prep to leave, rechecking medical and fire supplies.

The colonel answered on the second ring. "Crafton, what can I do for you?"

"I need your crew." Scott gave coordinates, fire specifications, and a brief account of the situation.

"I'll coordinate with the rangers and send a water drop and a crew of hot shots. They should be there in about twenty-five minutes. It'll take me about an hour to get to your position, but I will give orders to follow your command until I arrive."

Twenty-five minutes. The cabin would be engulfed in flames by that time. He needed to get in there and get Paige out.

"Thank you, sir." Scott barely kept his voice from shaking.

"Keep an eye on that fire," the colonel began.

"Bring all of our troops home." Scott finished.

He pocketed his cell phone and turned towards Rachel. "Bring up the thermal imaging of the cabin again."

"We still only have movement of one person inside. And they haven't moved far."

Paige. There was no way of knowing for sure, but his gut told him that she was still alive.

"I'm going in for her. The water drop won't get here in time to save the cabin. I need to get her out of there before that happens."

"I'm going with you." Agent Wilson was taking off his suit jacket.

"No. I'm not taking a civilian into a wildland fire. You have no fire experience."

"I'll go." Mateo stepped forward and started going through the bag with one hand, looking for fire gear.

Scott put a hand on his arm to still his progress. "I need you to stay here and watch the fire. You need to be my eyes." He pointed to the drone screen in the other hand. "If the fire shifts or the wind changes direction, I need you to tell me. Everyone should be safe here, but if that wind changes, I need someone who knows how to read a fire to get these two out of here."

Steely determination filled the young man's eyes and he rose to his full height. "I will be your eyes. Go get her, sir."

Scott jumped into the UTV and took off towards the cabin. The arid smell of smoke thickened the air as he drew closer to the back side of the cabin. Scott repositioned the wet rag around his nose and mouth while he sent a silent prayer that smoke wouldn't steal the breath from the woman he loved.

"Wind direction has switched to south southwest. The fire is creeping towards the creek bed. What is the ETA of the hot shots?" Mateo's voice came through the coms. Calm. In control. He would make an excellent fire commander one day.

"We have about fifteen more minutes until the crew gets to the drop zone."

"Copy....direction...Over." The coms were beginning to cut in and out. He figured this would happen the closer he came to the fire.

"Mateo, repeat that last one."

Static met him as the cabin came into view. He would get Paige and then move away from the flames to get radio signal again. The fire was roaring in the distance and the heat skidded along his skin from here. As long as the wind continued to blow in the opposite direction, he had time to get them both to safety.

Throwing the UTV into neutral, Scott dismounted and flew up the porch steps. The front door was left open a crack, and he peered inside to try and take in the situation before barging into the room. If the man had set a trap, he would be useless to Paige if he was too injured to do anything.

The cabin was small and from the opening in the door, he could see a figure laid out on the floor and someone bound to a chair laying on its back. He would recognize that hair anywhere. Paige. Just the sight of her filled his lungs with hope. He checked the rest of the door frame and what he could see of the cabin. There were no trip wires or traps that were visible.

"Paige."

She whipped her head towards the door as tears filled her eyes. "Scott, you came."

"Can you see any traps or other surprises that I should know of?"

"I don't see anything." Coughs wracked her body. "Marcus has been out cold since the other guy knocked him over the head. I'm not sure he's even alive."

"Hold on. I'm coming in." Scott moved to Marcus first. There was no pulse. "May God have mercy on your soul," he whispered as he made his way over to Paige, unsheathing his knife as he went.

"Let me help you." He sliced through the remaining two ties. Once free, Paige plowed into his arms. He caught her and held on tight. As much as he wanted to stay right there, he needed to get them out of here.

The wind stirred the curtain of the window by the door. The wind had changed directions again, which meant the fire was coming right for them. One small spark lit the curtain into blazes. It wouldn't be long until the whole cabin was inflamed.

"We need to save Marcus." Paige pulled on his hand.

"There is no time. He's dead." Scott brought out another rag. "Put this around your mouth and nose. It'll help with the smoke."

Once her cloth was in place, he led her outside to the UTV. The roof of the porch burst into flames above their heads as they ducked and jumped off the steps. The trees around them were going up, blocking their retreat.

"Mateo. Rachel. Can anyone hear me?" Static was the only response he could hear. The fire sounded like a freight train barreling down on them.

"We need to find a spot to dig in and deploy the shelter."

Paige's eyes were wide and unfocused. He got right in front of her face.

"Paige, I need you to focus. We will survive this, but I need you to listen and do everything I say."

She blinked once. Twice. And finally looked at him. "What do you need me to do?"

"That's my girl. We need to dig a hole deep enough for the two of us. There is help on the way, but we need to stay alive until they get here."

She started nodding her head. He gave her the collapsible shovel in his gear as he went for the spare in the UTV. They made quick work of the hole in the ground. The fire grew louder, taunting them that death was coming. The air was harder to breathe and he knew that they needed to be in the shelter before it was too late.

"Lay down with your head in the depression there." She looked at him with fear in her eyes. "I will lay on top of you and pull the shelter on top. I will protect you. I promise."

She grabbed him behind his head and gave him a strong, quick kiss, then dove into the dirt. He couldn't stop the smile even if he wanted to. Once they survived this, he would want a repeat performance. One where he would kiss her back.

Opening the shelter, he tucked his feet into the end and secured the part closest to the wall of flames. He pushed himself on top of Paige, careful to cover her smaller frame with his body. He pulled the top of the shelter over their heads and pinned it to the ground with his elbows and gloved hands.

In all of the fires that he fought during his time as a wildland firefighter, he hadn't had to deploy one of these shelters. The stories told by survivors didn't come close to describing how terrifying the situation was. There was only a thin layer of material between them and a fire that would turn the air superheated to the point that they could burn their lungs beyond use. Not to mention the toxins released by the flames themselves and the fact that the fire consumed all of the oxygen around it.

He whispered in her ear, "It will get loud and really hot, but try to take slow shallow breaths as close to the ground as you can."

"I'm scared, Scott." The shake in her voice tore at his heart.

"I know, sweetheart. Lord, we could use some of your providence right now. Be with us and protect us." Scott started quoting his father's favorite Psalm "'The Lord is my shepherd...'"

The familiar words calmed Paige's shaking and he could hear her whisper them in turn. The sound of the wind and fire made it difficult to hear one another, but he continued with the scripture. It brought him focus as the shelter shook and threatened to be ripped from his grip. He pinned her harder into the ground.

The heat from the material flickered only inches above his jacket. The shelter was only meant for one person.

With two underneath, he was much closer to the top than was designed.

"Please, Lord, send us some of those still waters." Above the roar of the fire, Scott made out another noise. "I think I hear a helicopter. Paige, help is on the way."

Before he could warn her, the whoosh of two hundred gallons of sludge surrounded them as the fire sputtered. The pain he felt everywhere couldn't dim the relief he felt knowing that the fire around them had been put out.

"Can we get out now, Scott?" Paige's question pushed the pain away temporarily.

"We need to wait a bit longer. I want to make sure it is safe to leave the shelter." *And I'm not sure I could move right now,* he admitted only to himself.

"Thank you for coming to save me." Paige twisted so that her face turned towards his. She pulled down her mask to reveal her cracked pink lips. Lips that he wanted desperately to kiss, but he needed to focus on what she was saying. "I wasn't sure if you would make it and I wouldn't get to tell you that I don't want to be alone anymore."

He wanted to touch her face, but he didn't dare move his arms yet. "Paige, you're not alone. I'm here for as long as you want me."

He couldn't resist her any longer. He closed the short distance between them, claiming her lips. She tasted of the earth, but he didn't care. She was alive and she was his. The soft moan from her made him deepen the kiss they shared. He wished he could move his hands and pull her close to show her that he wasn't going anywhere.

The sound of the helicopter filled the air, pulling him back to their reality. Scott braced for another pummeling of water on his back, but the pain never came. He sent a small prayer of thanksgiving. He wasn't sure his body could have taken another beating. They had made another pass a few yards away from their current location. Hopefully, the fire would be under control soon.

Once the helicopter sound faded into the distance Scott moved to release them from the shelter. "I'm going to pull back the shelter. It should be cool enough out there now. Cover your mouth again and we'll make the hike out to safety."

As if thinking about the rest of the team could summon them out of thin air, Mateo's voice came across the coms unit still in his ear.

"Chief, this is Mateo. Can you hear us? Over."

Scott pulled back the shelter the rest of the way and pressed the button to activate his side of the coms. "Mateo, this is Scott. I was able to secure myself and Paige in a fire shelter before the flames overtook us."

"Good to hear your voice, sir. A group of hot shots have parachuted to the area you indicated before you went in and the water drop was relocated over your position."

"You did good, Mateo. Thank you. Paige and I are going to have to hike out. Our UTV didn't make it." The charred vehicle sat in the middle of the darkened landscape. How close they came to burning to death hit him with enough force that his breath stalled for a moment. *Thank you, Lord, for protecting us.* He looked at Paige. *And for giving us a chance with each other.*

Paige circled her arms around his waist, "Let's get out of here."

He winced at her touch.

"I'm sorry. Are you hurt?" She pulled back, looking him over for injuries.

"200 gallons of sludge was dumped over top of us. It hurt a bit." He tried to chuckle, but the movement made all of his muscles spasm at once. "I'm going to feel that one for a while."

She draped his arm around her shoulder. "Let me help you."

Scott's pride wanted to pull back, but the help was making it easier to stand. "Fine, but only because I get to hold you close." He raised his eyebrows twice and gave her his best flirtatious grin.

"Did anyone tell you that you were a terrible flirt?"

"You're the only one that I've flirted with in over a decade." He winked.

She giggled, actually giggled. "Alright, Flyboy, let's get you out of here so I can check you out."

"As long as you are the one checking me out, I don't care where we go."

"You are terrible." She rolled her eyes.

"She's right. That was terrible, dude." Mateo's words made him stop short.

"How much of that did you hear?" Scott asked and then pointed to the coms in his ear when Paige gave him a questioning look.

Mateo laughed and said. "Enough to know how out of your league you are with Paige."

"Well, that may be true, but I've got the prettiest girl in my arms, so I'm not going to focus on my flirting game right now."

"Rachel wants me to tell you that she called in an ambulance. We'll take you to the cabin on our UTV. Agent Wilson has started to hike back already to get better reception to call in everything."

"We'll meet up with Wilson back at the cabin."

Paige's head snapped up at the mention of Wilson's name. "I need to talk with Agent Wilson as soon as possible. Agent Hunter was the one who hired Marcus to steal my work."

Chapter 21

"**A**GENT HUNTER? ARE YOU sure?" Scott asked with concern in his voice. She had never been so happy to see anyone in her life when he called her name through the door. He came for her. Just like he said he would. All she wanted to do right now was curl in a ball under her soft downy comforter on her memory foam mattress in her camper. Yes, she could sleep for hours, especially if a strong airman was holding her close.

A cough from Scott brought her out of her daydreaming. "Yes. Marcus and Pyroeis both mentioned Hunter as the man who hired them to steal my work. When they couldn't take the drive, they took me."

"You saw Pyroeis?"

"More like saw the outline of the man, but no details. He was always shrouded in shadows and spoke in a deep voice except when I mentioned God bringing beauty out of ashes. Then he yelled like a crazy man losing his grip on reality." She put her hand on his chest. "And, Scott, he is a crazy man, or at least unhinged. He's obsessed with fire.

He waxed on about how it cleanses the earth to rid it of evil." She shivered. "It was creepy."

Scott tightened his grip around her shoulders. She was supposed to be the one supporting him, not the other way around.

"You are safe now. We will deal with Hunter and Pyroeis once we get back to the cabin." He curled his arm so that she was now facing him with only inches between them. "I thought I had lost you." His sincerity fought to undo her tough exterior. He rested his forehead on hers. He smelled of smoke, sweat, and dirt. Not the most tantalizing of smells, but it meant they were alive and she would never take that for granted. A tear traced down her cheek.

"Oh, man. Don't cry." He brushed the moisture away.

She blinked rapidly to hold back the water works. "I wasn't sure that God heard my prayers to have you find me in time." He wrapped her in a hug. "But I never felt alone. Yours and Hank's words kept filling my mind. Reminding me that God was with me."

She pushed back on his chest not wanting to break the embrace, but also needing to see his face.

"I knew with all my heart that you would find me and God would give us a chance to see where this relationship was going."

Scott's eyes widened slightly. Shoot, she was probably too forward and scared him with her talk of voices and relationships.

"Scott, I..." All excuses and apologies died in her throat as Scott's lips claimed hers. This time there was no shelter to hold in place and his hands slid across her shoulders and pulled her close. She melted into his embrace and worked her fingers through the hair at the nape of his neck, pushing the hard hat off of his head. Her touch seemed to ignite a passion deep within him.

A low moan rumbled in his chest as he broke away. Breathing hard, he slipped his hands to her waist. "That went much better than last time."

She couldn't help it, she threw her head back and laughed. "I would have to agree." The motion caused her head to swim a bit, but she was too happy to care.

"You two will have to practice mouth to mouth later." Rachel's voice was like a splash of cold water. Scott loosed his grip on her, but didn't let her go the whole way. Something she didn't want to happen either. "We need to get both of you back to the cabin to be checked over by paramedics and you can give your statements to Agent Wilson."

Paige looked past Rachel to see Mateo waving with a boyish grin on his face, standing next to another UTV. Thank goodness for the vehicle. Adrenaline crash was taking hold and she wasn't sure how long she could keep her eyes open.

Maybe Scott could feel her waning energy, because next thing she knew, she was swept up in his arms.

"Put me down. I can walk and you are injured," she said weakly. What was wrong with her?

"I'm not letting you go," Scott murmured in her ear.

She must have been more exhausted than she thought because she felt herself sigh and rest her head on his muscled shoulder. "Promise?"

"I promise."

She faded in and out of consciousness as they bounced down the trail towards the cabin. Scott held her in his arms the whole time until he gently laid her on a couch. Then there was only blissful darkness as she fell into unconsciousness.

When her eyes flickered open again, Kevin Jones' face filled her vision.

"Hey there, Paige. We are on our way to the hospital."

"Paige." Scott's rough voice was beside her. He lifted the oxygen mask off of his face and smiled at her. "I'm still here."

Paige smiled, or at least in her mind she did before the darkness claimed her again. Looked like she couldn't flee from the darkness, but this time with Scott holding her hand, she wasn't afraid.

The air inside the shelter was getting hot. Too hot. It was hard to breathe and she couldn't move because Scott lay on top of her. They needed to get out of there or they would die.

The rapid beeps of a heart monitor pulled her out of the dream and a gasp left her lips.

A gentle hand laid on her arm. "It's okay," Paola's soft voice crooned. "It was only a nightmare."

As she blinked, the familiar face came into focus. As much as she was happy to see the woman who had become like a mother to her, Scott had promised to be here. "Where's Scott?" she croaked.

"They almost had to sedate him to get him to agree to a chest x-ray." Paola shook her head. "He didn't want to leave your side."

Paige relaxed a bit into her hospital bed. They had made it to the hospital safely, but she needed to tell Agent Wilson about Hunter before the man disappeared.

"I need to speak with Agent Wilson."

"Honey, you suffered from smoke inhalation and were dehydrated to the point of passing out." She patted her hand. "You need to rest."

"It's important. The man who hired Eros may get what he wants if I don't speak with Wilson now." She put as much bite behind her words as she could, but she was weakened from being captured.

Paola rose from her bedside chair, uncertainty waging in her eyes. "Alright. I will be right back, but if you need anything, hit the call button and I personally will come running."

Paige nodded and exhaled hard when Paola left the room.

A moment later a quiet click sounded, telling her that someone had entered her room.

"That was fast. I'm glad she found you...Agent Hunter? How?"

The balding man swept the curtain back to expose the gun, equipped with a silencer, pointed right at her.

"It's a shame really. You are so talented and would have done great things for good ol' Uncle Sam. But I can't have that pretty little brain of yours telling my superiors about my side business," the man sneered.

"How are you going to explain away the bullet hole while I'm in a hospital?"

He barked a bitter laugh. "This is only Plan B. No, I think that a heart attack because a nurse messed up your meds is a more realistic way for you to go. Don't you think?"

"Is that how you killed Rollands?" She wasn't sure if he actually did kill Rollands, but she needed to buy more time until someone came back. Again. This whole being taken hostage thing was getting old.

"Rollands was getting too close to putting the pieces together." He pulled a vial from his pocket. "It's a shame, really, because he was one of the best agents we had at DCIS."

"So now what? Are you going to sell my program to the highest bidder?"

"Don't be ridiculous. The program is useless without the camera tech to go with it. No, I'm going to sell your calculations so that people can adapt to the changing technology. It's not always about stealing the tech as it is about making it useless." He drew some liquid into a syringe.

"And this way the tech doesn't disappear, which prevents red flags pointed right at you."

"See? Brilliant. Now lay still. This won't hurt much."

"Paige, Paola said you wanted to talk with me." Agent Wilson froze in mid step. "Hunter? What are you doing here?"

Zeroing in on the syringe in his hands, Wilson took a quick step towards him. The energy in the air zapped with tension as Paige watched the two men stare at each other.

"Answer the question, Hunter," Wilson growled.

"I am your commanding officer. You need to stand down."

Paige blinked and Wilson tackled Hunter. The two agents were wrestling to gain control of the syringe and gun when she heard a voice coming from the hall.

"I'm not going back to another room. Give it to someone else. I'm staying with Paige."

Scott burst through the door as the gun skidded across the floor and stopped at his feet. He scooped up the piece and bellowed, "It's over, Hunter."

Wilson used the momentary distraction to knock the syringe out of Hunter's hand. The older agent slumped to the floor, defeat clouding his face. Wilson didn't miss a beat, but flipped Hunter onto his stomach and secured his hands behind his back.

"Now, would someone catch me up?" Wilson's shoulders rose and fell with heavy breaths.

Scott flipped the gun around and handed the butt end to Wilson. "Paige has a story to tell you and Hunter's actions here will back it up."

Scott filled his lungs for the first time since coming into the room. He walked over to Paige, who looked so small laying in the oversized bed. She patted the space next to her and attempted to make room for him. He sat next to her on the bed and intertwined their hands. He was not leaving her side again.

She laid her head on his shoulder and sighed. Wilson dragged Hunter from the room and gave instructions to a uniform in the hall to take the man to holding until he came for him.

"You just couldn't stay out of trouble, could you, Doc?" Scott kissed the top of her head.

"It was a good thing Agent Wilson came to my rescue." She pulled away and gave him a wry smile.

To see that smile made a thousand sleepless nights and all the worry in the world seem inconsequential. This strong, courageous woman was worth walking through any nightmare life could throw at him.

Reappearing in the room, Wilson walked towards her bed. "You've had an eventful day. Why don't you start at the beginning when you're ready." Wilson took the seat at the foot of her bed and waited.

Paige tightened the grip on his hand and started recounting what happened, starting with the explosion at his parents' house. When she told them about how her clothes were changed while she was unconscious and how they made her pose for pictures, his gut twisted and he had to resist the desire to punch through a wall.

"You seem like a capable woman, why did you not make a run for it while you were out of your bonds?"

She looked at Scott. "They threatened to take Rachel and sell both of us." Turning her attention back to Agent Wilson, she continued. "I knew that Scott and Rachel were looking for me, and so I bought as much time as I could."

Her faith in him and Rachel filled him with peace. He leaned over and gave her a kiss on her head. He knew it wasn't professional, but he needed her to know that her trust and faith in him was appreciated.

She continued recounting what happened to her and the dynamic between Pyroeis and Marcus.

"Are you saying that this Pyroeis was Marcus' partner?"

"I don't think that they were necessarily working together. Pyroeis seemed like he was there to make sure Marcus didn't screw up again. Did Rachel give you my program?"

"It hasn't left my side." He patted the inside pocket of his suit jacket. "I will personally deliver it to DC once I'm done here. With Hunter caught in the act of trying to kill you, I am just looking to tie up loose ends. Will you be returning to DC with me?"

Paige looked at Scott. "I think I might stay a while. See what God has planned for me."

Happiness bubbled inside of Scott's chest that exploded when she gave him that full smile of hers.

"Understood." Wilson broke the moment. "You said that Pyroeis was there to make sure Marcus didn't screw up again. What made you say that?"

"Pyroeis said that Malinoe thought Marcus was weak right before he killed him by knocking him on the head with a blow torch. I think not being able to find my completed research put Marcus in a tight spot with Malinoe. They are the ones pulling all of the strings."

"Did you hear or see either Pyroeis or Malinoe?"

"No. Pyroeis was hooded and stayed in the shadows and both men only mentioned Malinoe. As far as I know, Malinoe was never in the cabin." She looked at Scott as if to ask permission to share what they knew of the criminal organization.

Scott filled in Agent Wilson on his family's search into Malinoe. The man was a seasoned agent and didn't show an ounce of surprise when Scott told them about the suspected human trafficking and stolen art.

"I have a friend at the FBI who sent out a bulletin to other agencies about something similar. If I remember correctly, the organization boasts that they can find you what you want for the right price. I'll reach out to him. He might have more questions for you."

"We will help however we can." Scott couldn't care who stopped these people as long as they were no longer able to continue in their malicious intentions. He didn't tell Wilson about Heather and he would hold his judgement on the amount of trust he had for this FBI agent before he let anyone know about the identity of their inside woman.

"If I need anything else, I will give you a call." Wilson took one of his business cards and wrote a name on the back. He gave Scott the card. "This is the name of the FBI agent I was telling you about. I hope you are able to work together to bring this organization down."

Scott heard the warning in the agent's voice. *Don't go vigilante.* Fine by him, but his father was never one to back down from a fight.

"These people are dangerous and clearly have high-powered clientele. Work within the law to make sure you keep everyone safe." Wilson's gaze slid to Paige. Scott gave the agent a solemn nod and a promise to himself to do his best to keep them all safe.

"I've been told you are a genius and clearly one tough lady. If you ever change your mind and want to join DCIS, just give me a call. I've got to go fill out a mountain of paperwork and hopefully find a digital trail so that when Hunter goes away for a long time, we might be able to take someone else down with him."

Wilson left the room and Scott relaxed his shoulders. He put his arm around Paige and pulled them back against the inclined bed.

"One thing today taught me is that I have strong feelings for you, Paige MacFarland."

"Mmmm. Such a romantic."

"You may not believe this, but I haven't dated anyone since I left New Freedom." Scott winced. "I'm a bit rusty."

"You're doing just fine, Flyboy." Paige's head settled onto his shoulder and he marveled at how well she fit against him.

He opened his mouth to try again to explain to her how much she meant to him when the soft rhythm of her breathing told him she had fallen asleep. A man could get used to moments like these. A great woman sleeping in his arms, a job that challenged him in all the right ways, and a renewed relationship with his family.

Epilogue

Two Weeks Later

It had finally rained for the last week, but today the sun shone brightly as almost the whole company showed up for their monthly training. Paige finished setting up the CPR dummies as Tucker's voice boomed from the other side of the firehouse bay. She still couldn't quite figure the man out. He was an excellent leader, most of the people in the company liked him, and all of them at least respected his authority when it came to training.

Right now, everyone was focused on the instructions he was giving about knots and creating a belay system when you had no harnesses.

Paige sighed. She was content and most importantly, no longer alone. She had a new job working with Kora as a computer analyst. Her job was to find people digitally, or at least evidence of people. After being taken herself, she wanted the opportunity to help find others, and Charles Crafton was eager to have her on board.

"I hope that sigh was a good thing." Scott put his arm around her waist and pulled her to his side. He was careful when at the firehouse not to show too much affection, but she knew how deep his feelings went, or at least she was beginning to understand.

She snaked her arm around his waist. "I was just thinking about how I'm not alone anymore, which makes me happy."

He gave her a slight squeeze. "I, for one, am glad you chose to stay. After training, everyone is going out for pizza, but I was hoping that you'd like to come over to my place to relax for a bit after we grab a bite to eat."

Since his parents' house was still in the process of being rebuilt, they had moved into the cabin with Rachel, and Scott was renting a small bungalow just on the outskirts of town.

"You know, for a man who is so confident in commanding his troops in an emergency situation, you seem nervous." She nudged him with her shoulder.

When he didn't answer she looked at him. Those blue eyes were so full of love and desire, she almost broke her promise to not kiss him at the station.

"You are the most amazing woman I have ever met. I know that you have lost so much already. I don't want to pressure you into anything, so I will wait for as long as it takes."

This man was more than she deserved. "There's no need to wait. My heart belongs to you, Scott Crafton. I love you."

The smile that she received in return made her knees go weak. "You're making it difficult to stick to our no kissing at the station rule," she joked.

Scott leaned closer. "Tucker is busy and I don't think he'd write us up."

"Chief, can I talk with you for a minute?"

Scott gave a soft growl. "I understand now why Tucker didn't want to work with that man. We will continue this tonight." He kissed her head and left to meet with the mayor.

Scott had meticulously typed out a full report on the company with areas they excelled in and areas they needed improvement. Tucker requested a rescue truck, complete with a river rescue trailer that they could hook up to if needed. The truck would allow them to get to the more secluded places outside of town faster. Since he was dreaming and wishing, Scott also put in for a helicopter to be shared throughout the county for the mayor to take to the county board of executives or to the governor. There were places, especially in this area of the state, that were remote, and getting units to them takes precious time.

Paige said a short prayer for him. Because of her time in DC, she was wary of all politicians, no matter how small the group that they governed.

"Hey, sis." Rachel wandered through the open bay doors.

Paige spun to face her. "You know that we aren't married yet. We aren't even engaged."

"I give it until the end of the month," Rachel stated without a doubt.

Paige's heart leaped. Was she ready to try and get married again? If it was to Scott, that would be a one hundred percent yes. A part of her heart would always belong to Hank, but she knew that Scott would cherish her and love her all the rest of her days. That truth tipped up her lips in a slow smile.

"Good to know you'll say yes." Rachel nudged her with her shoulder, then turned somber. "I called Agent Wilson this morning for an update."

"It's Saturday. You should have let the poor man have a day off."

Rachel snorted. "He told me to call him today so that he could fill me in outside of the office."

Paige didn't like the ominous turn this conversation was taking.

"He said that Hunter will stand trial for a long list of offenses. Murder, kidnapping, extortion to name a few. Turns out he has been using Malinoe for a while to find people he considered a threat to his side business of selling government secrets."

Rachel paused and Paige knew what she was about to say would rock her.

"Hank's death was Hunter's doing. One of the men in Hank's unit had proof of Hunter's dealings and was going to take it to the authorities once he got stateside. Malinoe's organization tracked him to Afghanistan and Hunter hired an assassin to take him out."

Paige's world tilted a bit. Not only did they put a stop to a crooked man, she had also found closure in Hank's death.

"Thank you Rachel," was all she could say.

"Also, I thought you would want to know that the cabin you were held in was owned by Melton Fox. Apparently, Stanley hadn't sold it yet."

Paige shivered. That cabin still haunted her nightmares although they were becoming less frequent.

"Wait." Paige snapped her fingers. "The day Rollands died, Stanley talked to me at the coffee shop while I waited. He said that Marcus told him about me. Marcus probably conned Stanley into letting him use the cabin."

"I'll let Agent Wilson know." Rachel took out her phone and sent out a text.

Paige knew she should be the one to be in contact with Wilson, but Rachel had taken it upon herself to be the liaison between the two. She figured it was Rachel's way to help.

"Have you heard anything from the FBI about the art found at the Zeits' house?" Rachel asked as she put her phone in her pocket. She didn't look at Paige though. Her eyes scanned the room as if looking for someone. Paige could recognize that look anywhere.

"Mateo is helping Scott set up for the circuit training out back." At Paige's statement, Rachel whipped her head around with her eyes wide.

Paige looked at her, challenging her to deny that was who she was looking for.

Rachel exhaled hard. "He is one of the few men that doesn't shy away from all of my...quirks."

Paige bit her lips, trying to hold back the smile that wanted to escape. "Well, from what I've seen, he's a good man."

"He is." Both women spun to see a slender woman with short, spiky dark hair that had a streak of red through the side-swept bangs. She wore black cargo pants, black boots, and a black wicking shirt that showed off her toned body. She looked intense and Paige's guard automatically went up.

"Who are you?" Rachel demanded.

"Don't worry, Rachel, I'm not here to hurt anyone. I don't do that kind of thing. Well, not in a physical sense."

"Heather?" Rachel's jaw dropped. "I didn't recognize you with the new hair. It looks good. A bit dark and brooding, but good."

Heather hitched up the side of her mouth. "Thanks." Heather reached out a hand to Paige. "We haven't officially met when you were conscious, I go by Kai now, but everyone around here knows me as Heather."

"Were you the one who changed my clothes?" Móraí would be appalled at her lack of social propriety, but Paige needed to know what happened while she was knocked out.

"Marcus, despite what he did, had a soft spot for you. He couldn't bring himself to touch you in that way, so I volunteered. It's what let me get the coordinates to send to Scott and Rachel." Heather lifted one shoulder. "If I could save one person from this life, I'm going to. No matter the cost to myself."

"Are you in trouble? We can bring you in. We can protect you." Rachel was getting louder and Paige put a hand on her arm to calm her down.

"It's nothing I can't handle"— Heather shifted her weight back and forth — "but thanks for the offer."

"Can I help you, ma'am?" Tucker's deep voice made Paige jump. "Didn't mean to scare you, Paige, just thought I would come see what all the commotion was about now that the company is out back with Scott and Mateo."

Heather looked as if she had seen a ghost. Her eyes were wide and she lost some color in her cheeks. She blinked and the momentary shock was gone.

"I'm Kai." When they shook hands a silent message passed between the two and Heather took in a sharp breath before wiping her hand on her pants.

"I'm Tucker. Are you new to town?"

Heather cut her gaze to Paige and Rachel, then said with a smile, "It's been a long time since I've come home, and one day I'd like to return for good."

"Well, when you return maybe we can get to know each other."

"I'd like that." Heather gave him a genuine smile.

Tucker took a card from his wallet and wrote on the back. "That's my personal number. When you come back, give me a call."

Paige had never seen Tucker even come close to flirting with a woman. He was usually all business.

"Kai." Paige emphasized her name to redirect her attention. "Was there something you wanted to tell us?"

Heather snapped her attention back to the women. "Tell Charles to be careful and lay low for a bit. I'll do what I can. Also, from what I can tell, Locklear is on the up and up."

"How did..."

Heather held up her hand to stop Rachel from asking. "Don't ask questions you don't want answers to. Stay safe and I'll be in touch." She turned to Tucker with another warm smile. "It was good to meet you, Tucker. I'm looking forward to a coffee date with you next time I'm in town." She gave him a wink and then disappeared around the corner of the building.

Paige looked at Tucker, expecting to see confusion or concern, but the grin on his face told of his growing interest in the mysterious woman.

"I'm not going to ask what that was about or who she actually was, but I should get out back. The last one to finish the circuit buys the pizza for the chief." Tucker jogged away.

"Huh," was all Paige could say.

"I know. I didn't realize that guy had it in him to flirt with anyone. It's not like women haven't noticed him, but he's never been interested." Rachel shook her head as if to refocus her thoughts. "I should go check in with Tylan about the art from the Zeits' place. He said he was doing surveillance this weekend. Hopefully, we'll get some more answers."

Rachel was working on her PI license and Tylan agreed to be her sponsor. Paige tugged on Rachel's arm to keep her from leaving. "Please be careful. Heather's warning was for Charles, but I think that it extends to all of Kora."

"I'll keep my eyes open."

Paige watched as Rachel walked down the street towards Main. She said a prayer that God would keep them all safe as they figured out all the players in this deadly game.

Sneak Peek
from Flare Up

The past they thought they'd escaped is coming for them...

Madysin Viruel barely escaped with her life while working undercover in El Salvador to stop the trafficking of young girls. Now back in New Freedom, she's determined to rebuild—but when the predators she once exposed track her down, the only person she can turn to is the man she's never stopped loving.

Private Investigator and volunteer firefighter Tylan Jamison has one priority—keeping his four-year-old daughter, Sari, safe. After his wife's tragic death, he vowed nothing from the past would ever touch her. But when his wife's past collides with his present, the threat to Sari becomes all too real.

Thrown together by danger, bound by an unshakable connection, Madysin and Tylan must face the shadows that haunt them both. Every step they take draws the enemy closer—and this time, losing could cost them everything.

Chapter 1

Candelaria de la Frontera
  El Salvador
  Her mind screamed to keep going, but her body was going to quit. A person could only endure so much bodily pain before it started to shut down to save itself.

Branches slapped her face and the soft ground cushioned her footfalls. She only needed to make it to the village where the friar would give her shelter.

This was not Madyson Viruel's first time stopping *el tren fantasma* from stealing girls into the night, but she should have anticipated that the men would eventually figure out her game plan.

The red roof of the church could finally be seen through the trees. She was almost to safety.

Her legs burned from the running, but the deep gash on the outside of her right leg is what made her want to fall in a heap and pray for God to take it all away.

Her run became more of a stumble as the pain clouded her mind. She needed to stay focused.

Get to safety. Make the call. Don't Die.

A tree root snagged her foot and the ground came up to her. A whimper escaped her lips.

She would die here.

No, she couldn't let that happen.

Lifting her head, she locked her gaze on the church. Only a few more yards. She could do this. She had to do this.

Gripping the tree she hoisted herself to almost standing. The rough bark cut into her skin, but she continued to use each passing tree to help her drag her leg.

A twig behind her snapped. They couldn't have found her.

A tall man appeared from behind a tree.

She screamed as loud as she could and stepped out on her right leg to run. Her leg was weaker than she thought and the weight of her body caused it to collapse.

Her head didn't hit the soft ground as it had moments ago, but made contact with a rock. The sharp pain seized her body as the darkness pulled her under.

"Help me...God please." She whispered as the world disappeared.

About the author

Lily J. Hann writes Christian romantic suspense novels that intertwine thrilling mysteries with messages of faith and love. A devoted wife and mom, she cherishes time spent exploring life's adventures with her husband and two sons. When she's not writing or adventuring, you'll likely find her curled up with a good book or enjoying a quiet moment with a cup of coffee. Lily lives in Maryland, where her family and faith inspire her stories.

Be sure to subscribe to her newsletter for all of the latest on upcoming books.

*Scan and subscribe
to Lily's newsletter*

Also by Lily Hann

<u>New Freedom Fire and Rescue</u>
Spotting the Fire
Flare Up (coming 2026)
<u>Seward Field Office</u>
Alaskan Family Ties (Re-releasing November 2025)
Alaskan Hero's Return (coming May 2026)

Visit www.lilyhannauthor.com for complete list of books
and ways to purchase all of your favorites.

www.ingramcontent.com/pod-product-compliance
Lightning Source LLC
Chambersburg PA
CBHW020402110726
47899CB00006B/1819